CAPITAL FARM

AND

OTHER FABLES

By Eric Blair

Eric Blair

ISBN-13: 978-0615627939

ISBN-10: 0615627935

You may contact the author at www.capitalfarm.org

Disclaimer

This is a work of fiction inspired by general American history. Any resemblance of any character in this work to actual and historical persons, places or events is coincidental.

To My Wife and Kids

CAPITAL FARM

Chapter One

Cato walked up the mountainside, above the rest, turned about, and sat down like a statue on top of a rock looked like a Hog. At the foot of the mountain, about a hundred-forty animals wait for him to sit. Then they sat or lay down, most of 'em. Ducks and Geese in the front row. Puppies play on the grass next to their parents. Behind them Cows and Horses and Foals eatin' grass.

When everyone was quiet, Cato the Great Dane spoke, but nobody heard him 'cause the Sheep begin to bleat:

This is my story,
This is my song,
Praising my Savior all the day long!

This is my story,
This is my song,
Praising my Savior all the day long!

Everyone sang it. Cows lowed it, Dogs barked it, Horses whinnied it, Ducks quacked it. In unison. And they knew. This had to be the place. The hymn is over.

"My friends," Cato says, "we are here."

Cries of thanks and praise. A Rooster crows, "Hallelujah!" instead of "Cock-a-doodle-do!" Everyone gives thanks to God.

"No human being," Cato went on, "not *one*, thought we would make it. None came with us. No help from them. We did it ourselves. Providence has smiled upon us."

"Remember the day we left Whiteacre? It rained -- all day. We waited and waited in the barn for Mr. George to say good-bye but he never came."

The Chickens clucked, Ducks quacked and Geese honked in agreement. They hated their owner Mr. George. Most eager ones to leave his farm. Religious, them Birds. Taught their children Birds was closer to Heaven 'cause they could fly. Other animals only jump. But them Birds could not agree among themselves about the Christian religion, that's fer sure.

Plymouth Rock Chickens, now, those Puritans disliked Doves. Doves were Quakers. You know – a different religion. Doves refused to hold church services with them Chickens, and vice versa. Now Leghorn Chickens were Baptists baptizing in water by immersion (see the Gospel of Mark) just like the Puddle Ducks and Geese. Baptists refused to hold services with either the Plymouth Rock Chickens or the Doves. Birds couldn't get along religiously.

Now they listen to Cato that steel-blue Great Dane tell how they traveled. One hundred forty-four animals. Small and old ones rode in wagons the Horses pulled. Most never been off Whiteacre before. They marched to the foot of a nearby mountain and stop for the night.

Next day they cross the mountains over the nearest pass. Other side of the mountains was barren. No white clouds just blue skies. Sun stung their eyes, poor animals. Orange dirt. Saltbushes. Found their way down to a dirt valley. At the bottom of the valley headed due west. By the end of the day, they travel ten miles.

That night was cold so Pigs build a fire. Smart animals, them pigs. Dogs sleep on the perimeter, sniffin' at the air. Pigs tend the fire. Everyone slept good.

Next day, walkin' in the desert, the landscape gets worse. They see Crucifixion Thorn, Angel's Trumpet, Devil's Claw. Nothin' but nothin' to eat. At sundown they all march single file down a dry riverbed. They had gone another twenty miles. Now they see Organ Pipe Cactus, Cheatgrass and Pepperweed. "I miss grass!" one animal whines by the campfire. "Do any green leaves grow in this desert?"

Around two in the mornin', Ghost-faced Bats fly into camp. Them Bats is chasin' Mormon Crickets fer food. The animals were scared of them Bats. Especially them Cows. Females and children hide under them wagons. Bats fly off. Night becomes quiet. Thunder rumbles in the distance. Raindrops drizzle. Strange creatures climbs up out of the dirt of the riverbed and scrambles up out of that wash. A cold gust of wind, and it rains like animals never seen before. And hail size of rocks.

Lightning cuts into Joshua Trees nearby. Bushes begin burnin'. They try to hide under wagons now but there warn't enough room for 'em all. Pigs and Dogs grab the good spots. Other poor animals soaked with rain, hit by hail, and water flash-floods down into the wash.

"Run!" someone shouted. They scrambles up and over the sides of the wash. Two wagons washed away. Four Chickens and two Sheep drownd. Wind whips rain every which way. Lightning slits the sky in two. Thunder rumbles reality.

Then it just stopped. Clouds leave. Myriad stars and full moon come out. Air is still cool, so they huddled together for warmth, tryin' to sleep. Didn't care what religion, color or species others were. Just tryin' to keep warm. Spadefoot Frogs squirm up through the dirt, keep 'em up rest of that night: "Kerokee, kerokee, kerokee!"

Next day, Doves spies the drownded Chickens and Sheep in the dirt. Them animals holds a funeral. Sing "What a Friend We Have in Jesus" and move west.

The landscape begins to change again third day. Pink sand. Stone arches, tall pillars. Nothin' in bright blue sky. For twenty-one days they travel at night. Too hot to travel days. Deadly heat. At dusk they sets out, purple ghosts walkin' upon stars -- and under them stars, too. The moon comes and the moon goes, but sand sparkles in the starlight. Stars above, stars below. Ever seen that? Animals walkin' 'mong stars. Wish I'd a been there....

One mornin', come sunrise, they camps on the lip of a big bowl a' sand. Marcia, youngest calf of the bunch, falls down into it. Broke her leg. She moos for help. Broke your heart. Mother couldn't save her. When it grows quiet, she is dead. Mother wept in the shade 'tween two wagons, under an awnin', waitin' for sundown to save her daughter. Turkey Vultures do not wait, and God knows they did not weep. Landin' in the hollow, Turkeys begin to tear the Calf and to eat. Some quarrel over the flesh. Marcia's mom couldn't wait. She dove down the hollow and drive 'em off. After half an hour she is dead, too. The desert sun, you know. Turkeys came back and picked 'em clean and flew off for water.

Come sundown the animals bury bones in the sand and held a funeral. Then they march west a-singin':

> How Firm a Foundation,
> Ye Saints of the Lord,
> Is laid for your faith,
> In His excellent word!
> What more can He say
> Than to you He hath said,
> To you, who for refuge
> To Jesus have fled?

Thirty days since they left Mr. George's farm.

On the thirty-first day, after a month of dirt and sand and death, they spies grass. Green grass! Hills of it. Miles of it. Risin' afore them into the dusk. Without a word, everyone ran, galloped or flew right to the grass. Come sunup they reached it. The Horses, Cows and Sheep ate it. Pigs and Dogs roll on it. They could travel days again, sleepin' under the star-spangled night.

On day number thirty-five, they hear thunder rumblin' from the north. No cloud in the sky, just dust risin' from earth. "Rain?" they asked, bumpin' into each other a-lookin' up at heaven fer answers. It grew louder, so everyone hid under and 'round the wagons again. Then a whole herd of Bison come runnin' round a hill straight for their wagons, heads a-bobbin' up and down, up and down a-chargin' like thunder. Thousands of 'em. Last second they veer off to either side and start eatin' prairie grass. Like the animals weren't even there. Ignorin' 'em. The Bulls dig wallows in the plain, piss in 'em and roll in their own pee. Others charge one another until one lost the fight. When Bulls mounted their Cows on the open plain it was too much for them animals. Birds shield their youngun's eyes with their wings. It warn't proper to see.

After an hour, Buffalo chief comes to visit. His herd was goin' west, he says, so they could all travel together -- if the animals wanted. They did and make plans to move the next day.

Later that day chief gave a party for the animals. He introduces 'em to his family and friends, elders of the herd. A group of young Buffalo dances.

"We have grazed these plains many years," the chief says when the dancing ended. "Summers we return to purple mountain. We graze. We do not farm. The Great Spirit in the sky has given land to all. Our spirits run like clouds to the Buffalo wallow of the Great Spirit in the sky when we die."

"Do you believe in God?"

"Whose God?" says the chief.

"The Creator," some animals say, "why, that's who!" But just then it began to rain, so the animals went back to their camp, and the chief goes back to his wallow.

Next day they give a gift to the chief, sacks full of grain.

"Thank you for your hospitality," they says. "This is our food. Please try it."

"On behalf of my herd," chief says, "I thank you." He draws the wagon of grain to the center of about ten thousand Bison. Then he pours the grain out on the prairie for all of them to eat. Old and young, Bulls and Cows, everybody tries the animals' strange-lookin' food. Then the Buffalo left. Time to move on to purple mountain, they says. Plan was for the Buffalo to lead the way, animals follow behind. But the animals doesn't follow. They stay in camp, quiet-like. A bellowin' fills the air, screamin' pain

"It's started," they says.

Them animals quietly broke camp and follow after the Buffalo. Comin' round a hill, they spy 'em lyin' on the prairie. They try to pick a way through the dead, but they run over some with wagons, there were so many of 'em.

Three days they follow the chief's directions to a purple mountain standin' lone in the middle of a plain. On the fortieth day they spy a single mountain peak alone in all its glory. Called it Mount Majesty, and the name stuck. Now they're a weepin' as Cato sittin' still as a statue tells of their journey. They all sing "A Mighty Fortress is Our God," and set up camp for the night at the foot of the mountain.

Chapter Two

'Twas no great surprise they make it to the purple mountain. Them animals were accomplished, they were. Cato, the Great Dane, measured almost six feet standin' on all fours and was damn strong. A "gentle-animal," he was, and a rich one, too. Never worked a day in his life. Not like you and me. That Dog owned a lot of land and slaves. Never smiled, though. Always talkin' serious, always talkin' 'bout his "honor" and his "interest." In charge of security for them animals. Sat straight up lookin' like a Roman statue carved out of rock. The Dog never moved! Incredible self-control. Sat for hours and hours without twitchin' his ears. And when he did move, quick as lightnin'. Steel blue blur. Cato. Didn't belong to one religion, neither. Believed in 'em all. Went to all services, even Catholic mass. Everybody welcomed Cato. You didn't say "no" when that big Dog holds your eyes and stares you down.

Now Merlin, he was a Yorkshire Boar. Hedonist, too. Loved to roll 'round in the mud for hours and hours. Felt good. Loved the lady Pigs, too -- and boy did they love him! Smart as whip, that Boar. Never been to school, just like Cato. That Pig was self-taught from readin'. Made money printin' books. From his inventions, too. Eye-glasses fer animals so they could see. Wore pair a' glasses himself. Mr. George's family liked Merlin a lot. Everybody liked him, 'ceptin' the Birds. They even hated his name: said it was pagan, unchristian. Didn't like he was friends with Mr. George, neither. And he was always flyin' kites to catch "electricity," Birds couldn't abide it. Birds said Merlin should'a been lookin' for God in heaven, not lightnin' in the skies. Now Merlin was the wise-crackingest Pig you ever meet. Loved to make them animals laugh, and Birds didn't like it 'cause they was religious. He didn't care. Didn't have no religion and he said so. Them Birds noticed. Wrote books on all subjects. You name it. Just *not* about religion. Most thought he was some kind of natural-born wizard just like his name, Merlin.

Now Scratch, he was a hedonistic Boar, too. Liked to roll 'round in the mud for hours. Owned a big library. Best in the world, some said. Got his name from scratchin' dirt with his knuckles when he spoke. (Birds called him Scratch 'cause he was a devil to them. Tusks not cut, red haired. *Au natural*. Published a New Testament. Took out the parts 'bout hell. Birds hated it. Called him devil.) Was as an architect, a surveyor, a lawyer and an inventor. One clever Pig. Knew Greek, Latin and French. Played his violin. Real "gentle-animal." Loved music. Never worked a day in his life. Owned slaves and he wrote *anti*-slavery books. Never did quite figure him out.

Then there was Jonah, Scratch's friend. Well, kind of. Toothless old Boston Terrier loved and hated Scratch. Both was lawyers. Jonah lived high up mountain where winters was cold. Didn't have much fur, neither. Didn't care. Spent time writin' his books 'bout politics. Made himself into a "gentle-animal." Owned a farm and loved his wife.

These three plus Cato was Mr. George's "Gov'nor's Council." Pigs and Dogs decided almost everything. Even if they didn't do the work. Pigs was clever. Dogs handled security. The Council split the whole Farm in half: lower part called South and upper part was called North. Cato and Scratch owned farms in the South. Merlin and Jonah lived up North. Dogs and Pigs ran things. There was a Chicken Farm South and Chicken Farm North; Horse Farm North and Horse Farm South. You get it. Farms was named after species. South grew cash crops. You know -- sugar, cotton, tobacco. North just corn and wheat. It was one big Farm.

First year was hard. Mr. George sent supplies, not as much as he promised or them animals needed. They plant crops, sure, but most of 'em fail. There weren't no humans to help. Winter comes on and it was colder and darker than they ever see. Nights last forever, and no candles. What little they harvested goes bad with mold. Couldn't eat it.

Luckily natives livin' on the mountain help them. A Red Deer called Sasha shows 'em where wild corn grew. They eat and are saved.

"Maize grows all year," she said. "There is no need to plant."

So relieved that they hold a feast with Sasha's herd and call it the Day of Gratitude. Rest from work and thank God for keepin' 'em alive. To this day we celebrate it.

The Farm grew in spite of hardship. Some animals die, most build a barn and survive. Hearin' about it, new animals come to the Farm. Some out of the wild. Foxes and Wolves. In five years time, the Farm is larger than Mr. George's farm.

Still, many who come cannot not pay their way. They sign contracts with Mr. George and rich gentle-animals who pay their way. In return, newcomers promise crops for five years.

Time passes, and newcomers fall deeper in debt. Crops fail. A black Ram named John buys his farm on credit from a Collie called Rolf. John loses the crop. Rolf wants to be paid so he sues John. Judge was a Boar named Mince. Come over from Mr. George's farm in the very beginning. He never studies law but Mr. George liked that Pig. Made him a judge. Mr. George says Pigs and Dogs is smarter than other animals.

"Sorry, your Honor," said John, a-tremblin' from hoof to horn, "but I lost my crop! There was nothin' I could do." He shakes his head. "I got nothin' left to pay." He breaks down in court, a grown Ram!

"Jack Ram," Mince squeals, "an animal's word is an animal's bond! Where would we be without promises? I sentence you to five years of hard labor. Rolf to be your master. May God have mercy on your soul!"

So now John despairs of ever getting' out of debt. One moonless night, he steals from Rolf's silo and gets caught. Mince is the judge again. He makes John's family appear in court, too.   Wife and four little Lambs. Black like John.

"Thievery!" the judge shouts. "Private property is sacred. I must make an example of you, John. I sentence you and your family to serve Rolf forever. You are now his property. May God have mercy on your souls!"

Thing was, this happened to lots of animals. They is all black, you know, black skin or fur or wool. So the other animals make it a law that black animals is slaves.   Some "white" animals disapproved but most didn't care. They think blacks is inferior. Birds in the South said black was evil.   White meant purity. "Children of Ham," those Birds call them slaves. "God cursed 'em. It's in the Bible." No sympathy at all. "The Bible allows slavery," they says. "Father Abraham owned slaves. Can't we?"

And slavery makes 'em money. Sugar, tobacco, cotton -- all need slaves. Three crops per year in the South. Only one in the North. No need for slaves up North.

But even free, animals couldn't sell their crops when they wanted to. Mr. George would not allow it. Everything is sent straight to George only. He sells their own crops back to 'em at a profit.   Or to human beings for a much better price. George sets the prices. Worst thing is animals wasn't allowed to use money neither. George pays 'em with crops from his own farm – whether they need 'em or not! Paid wheat to them that was growin' wheat, corn to them growin' corn. Money was so hard to come by common animals can't make a livin'. Many fall into debt. Black ones is made slaves.

Chapter Three

Now Mr. Pierre, he hated George. And Mr. George, he hated Pierre just as bad. Only thing they agreed on was how much they hates each other. Mr. P., he builds a farm on the north face of Mt. Majesty, just to spite Mr. G. Then he makes friends with them natives. You know, Red Wolves, Red Deer, and Bighorn Sheep. They attack Mr. George's animals but good. Some die. Somethin' has to be done, so Mr. George sends Cato to kill Pierre. He takes ten big Dogs and they set out on a trek round the purple mountain. Through virgin forests. Clear lakes, pristine streams. Cato seen nothin' like it before. Big country. Big trees. Them Dogs falls in love with the mountain. Lappin' ice-water in the big Quiet.

Three days walkin' 'n they find Pierre. Come dark, they creeps in real close and hides in the bushes. A bonfire's a-burnin' in front of a brown barn. Pierre was just a squat man with black hair. Speakin' to Bighorn Sheep and Red Deer. Men listenin' in.

But it's a trap. Red Wolves come up behind them Dogs and kill 'em 'ceptin' the Great Dane. Pierre likes Cato 'cause he doesn't beg fer his life. Sends Cato back with a message: War. Winner takes the mountain. Cato walks home alone.

News spreads quickly. Them animals want war, but Mr. George sends no men. Now Pierre got plenty men -- and guns. Plus the Deer, Bighorn Sheep and them Red Wolves. They leads Pierre's men by shortcuts. Things go bad. Animals die. Might have been the end of the Farm – if Mr. George didn't die himself. His liver done it. Drank too much. Mr. George, Jr. inherits Whiteacre and the war with Pierre.

First thing Jr. does is come to the Farm in person – hundred men with him. Builds a house in the center of Pig Farm South and moves in.

Governors Council meets every day. Hires new men to patrol the desert. They burns Pierre's wagons. Men drivin' wagons for Pierre took into custody. Pierre's Farm runs short on supplies, so his men begin' killin' Red Deer fer food. Them natives turn on Pierre. He begins losin' battles 'gainst Jr. Jr.'s men shoot them Wolf packs on the frontiers and torch Pierre's mountain farm. Pierre surrenders. Leaves that part of the mountain forever. The war is won! Animals and men celebrate all over the Farm by shootin' off guns.

Peace and prosperity last a good while. Land is cheap. Red Deer and Bighorn Sheep pushed off the mountain. The Farm grows bigger year by year. Animals with land get rich 'cause Jr. lets 'em use money now. Jr. keeps his house on Pig Farm and a hundred men North and South. The animals feed and clothe 'em for nothin' 'cause they won the war. But most animals want those men to go home. Enough Dogs on the Farm to keep order, they say. "We don't need human beings anymore."

After three months, Jr. owes his men pay for the war, so he makes every animal pay tax. All animals was required to give a third of everything they grow. Then he starts tellin' animals what crops they can grow. If an animal disobeys, Jr.'s men take the crops and threw the offender in jail -- or eat 'em as food, if they wants.

Time passes. In spite of Jr.'s rules, animals grow rich. They have children and settle the land. Most tolerate the men but resent 'em, too. Cato complains to Jr., so Jr. replaces the Governors Council with twenty sheriffs all over the mountain. 'Course the animals pay the sheriffs' salaries. Men do nothin' but collect taxes from animals since there are no more threats to the Farm. Buffalo, Bighorn Sheep, Red Deer, Red Wolves, even Mr. Pierre, all gone.

Comes as a great shock to them animals when Jr. dies. Travelin' 'cross the desert a Rattlesnake bit him. So Mr. George, III inherits Whiteacre. Animals call him "Third." He never visits the Farm. Third refuses to cross the desert and gets his information from sheriffs on the Farm. Now them sheriffs cheat and abuse animals. They blame everything on the animals and call 'em "lazy, filthy beasts." Then Third up and decides the Farm should not spread to the western side of the mountain 'cause the sheriffs say so. Them animals was mad. They say the sheriffs want the land for themselves and start callin' young Mr. George "the Terd." Then men kill some animals to make an example of 'em. What a mess!

"Something must be done," growls Jonah. Cato, Merlin, Scratch and Jonah meet at night. Full moon's hangin' low in the sky. No lights. George made a curfew. No animals allowed out. Fifty new men hired on the Farm to keep order.

"We are no match for George's men," says Cato, "too many guns."

"We have rifles," said Scratch, kickin' up dirt with them knuckles. "It's cannon most animals are afraid of."

"What news, Dr. Merlin?" says the Great Dane to the old Hog. "Will Pierre give us cannon or not?"

Merlin sighs, pushes his glasses on better with his knuckles and says, "We have ten small cannon already. Pierre will give us more – and men – if we prove we can win."

"Then we must win so we can win," said Cato, snuffin' the wind fer spies.

"Are the cannon secure?" barks Jonah. "Are they safe?"

"On my farm," grunts Merlin.

"Then what remains to be done?" says Scratch, a-pokin' at the dirt again.

"That's my area," says Jonah. "I will convene an Assembly to address George's closure of Horse Farm North. At the Animal Assembly I will come out for animal independence!"

"As will I!"

"And I!"

"And I," growls Cato. He thinks he hears someone a-comin'. An animal not a man.

"I will inform Pierre of our plans in person," says Merlin.

"Jusq'au bou!" grunts Scratch.

Each walks off a-listenin' fer spies in the dark.

George does have spies on the Farm, Rats and Birds never quite accepted by them animals. They tell men there are cannons hid on Merlin's farm. George orders his men to steal them cannons immediately. Soon as thirty men set out, Geese ya-honk the alarm. Oxen leave off plowin' fields. Pigs stop rootin' truffles. Dogs stop their huntin'. Everyone to Merlin's barn but quick. Them cannon are hauled to safety before the men arrive. Local Militia waitin' for 'em. To reach Merlin's farm they gots to cross the bridge over the Restless River. Ten small cannon are loaded by animals and aimed at that bridge.

Now that bridge was wood beams and rafters. When the last man steps onto the bridge animals open fire. "Kaboom!" "Baboom!" Roof splinters as shot shreds it. Shots land behind 'em, drivin' men forward where animals is waitin' for 'em in ambush. Men rush 'cross the river droppin' rifles. Animals spring out from behind trees. Fifty growlin' Dogs at men's throats while Pigs knock 'em to ground. Down men is easy to kill. The banks of the Restless run with blood.

But ten men gathered in a circle, no time to reload. They keep them animals off with swords and knives, but they's surrounded. Puddle Ducks flies over and shits in their eyes makin' 'em blind. Them Dogs see their chance. They bite them men's hands makin' 'em drop weapons. Pigs drag the dropped weapons off, and the men is unarmed. One by one they fall. Now the bridge over the Restless is a-burnin'. Soon it is gone.

One man escaped! Skinner, the leader. He runs along the river screamin' for help. Two Golden Retrievers run after him. He kills 'em with a dagger from his belt. Others are after him. Skinner's a big man, but he can't fight so many alone. He drops the knife and falls to his knees beggin' fer mercy. Them animals circle round him and start movin' in.

"Stop!" barks a voice from outside the circle. It's Cato.

"This man is my prisoner. Do not bite him!"

The circle opens. Cato walks to the man down on his knees and looks down at his face.

"He killed my friends," one Dog growls. "The human dies!"

"Leave him alone or you fight *me!*" says Cato, without movin'.

But the bloodlust is too strong. Two Golden Retrievers jump at Cato. He catches one, a-crushin' its windpipe while hittin' the other one with his shoulder. The first falls to the ground dead and the other one run off scared. Cato don't chase after him. Skinner is taken into custody as prisoner of war. And nobody disobeyed an order from Cato ever again.

News of defeat reaches Mr. George III. So begins the War of Rebellion 'tween the animals and Mr. George III.

Meanwhiles, hidden on Pig Farm North, the Animal Assembly meets. Every species sent delegates. They vote Cato commander-in-chief of their Animal Army. His lieutenant was Snapper, a Red Fox come in out of the wild to Dog Farm North. Snapper studied Latin and Law and Business. Like other animals he joins the Army to fight for animal independence.

Now George's strategy was to cut the Farm in half by occupyin' big farms up North. That way his men could be fightin' downhill as they move South. But Cato won't fight George's men in the open 'cause them animals ain't got no guns. Cato and Snapper only spring ambushes 'gainst the men as they march through the woods on the mountain.

Now the Assembly keeps tellin' Cato to free Horse Farm North from George's men. But the Great Dane don't have enough cannons. Meanwhile, the Assembly does not supply the Army "basic necessities." Soldiers fightin' without pay, food, guns or ammunition. How can you win a war like that? And the Assembly hadn't yet voted for animal independence!

"My friends,' barks Jonah in the Assembly. "George III seized my home and my land. I am an outlaw. Horse Farm North is overrun by humans. Did we not come to this mountain to escape human beings? George has severely restricted our industries; restricted our farming; restricted our settlements in favor of heathens. Our assemblies are outlawed and taxes have been levied upon us without our vote."

"Are we no better than slaves?"

"I and mine are George's slaves in the very Promised Land which I discovered and settled. And did I cross the desert for that?"

"My sole purpose in coming here was for my children to live free. Therefore I move this Assembly to vote for animal independence *now*!"

Many delegates to the Assembly voiced their approval. But a Dove now flew down from a nearby tree to address the Assembly. It was Elijah, a

Quaker.   He worries that George'll crush the Rebellion. And as a Quaker he's a pacifist.   He waits for everybody to quiet down. Then he speaks.

"I am as loyal to our Farm as any here," said Elijah. "Is independence worth more blood? How many will die before there is peace? And who will rule if Mr. George does not? I am not convinced animal independence will work!"

He flies back to the top of the tree.

A young Pig named Hampson stands up to speak. "It makes no sense to discuss matters in the abstract. Let us designate committees to write recommendations regarding these issues. Issue one: animal independence. Issue two: alliances with men. Issue three: the form of government we should adopt if reconciliation proves impossible.   I move we choose members of committees now! They will report back to us in a week."

So the Animal Assembly, over Elijah's protest, appointed teams to work on issues. Merlin, Jonah and Scratch are chosen to work on the issue of animal independence.

"You write the report," growls Jonah to Scratch. "I have not the skill."

"How do you figure that?" says the Pig.

"I am universally despised. I am not from the South. You are ten times the writer I am. I know."

"What about Dr. Merlin here?" asks Scratch, kicking at the dirt, turnin' to the other Hog. "Your books have been well received."

"I shall be happy if only to edit it and make constructive criticisms," winked Merlin adjustin' his glasses again.

"There is no one else to write it," barks Jonah. "You are the greatest scholar of us all. Tell us *why* animal independence cannot wait."

"Then it seems I am caught in a trap!" Scratch oinks a-laughin'.

"Begin immediately."

"Shall we meet back here in three days?"

Three days later, Scratch shows Merlin and Jonah this draft:

EXPLANATION OF INDEPENDENCE

Sometimes animals and human beings must go separate ways. In spite of history, in spite of traditions, animals must be true to their own Natures and to the God who created Nature. Nevertheless, the world still requires an explanation as to why animals and human beings should farm separately and independently. Every animal knows that every creature was created equal and that God gave to every creature eternal rights including, but not limited to, Life, Liberty and the pursuit of Happiness.

To ensure these rights, human beings and animals may choose whom they work for, so that every employer derives authority from the consent of his voluntary employees. That when any Farm becomes destructive of these ends, it is the right of animals to alter or abolish it, and to start a new Farm according to principles guaranteeing their Happiness and Safety. It is natural that animals continue under a yoke to which they are used, but when they are continually abused for the purpose of subjecting them to humanity's tyranny, it is their right, it is their duty, to throw off the yoke of man's authority and to themselves provide for their future prosperity.

Such has been the patience of these farms; and such is the necessity which forces them to found their own Farm. The acts of the present Head of the George family are a history of injuries and usurpations for the sole purpose of establishing an absolute tyranny over these farms. Let the facts speak for themselves.

Here Scratch listed the offenses of Mr. George III, such as evicting animals from their barns, taxation without representation and dissolving animals' local assemblies.

Merlin and Jonah read it. Then they read it again. When they started a third time, Scratch stops knucklin' the soil and speaks up.

"Well? What do you say?"

"Fabulous! It is one of the greatest documents ever penned," says the Boston Terrier.

"I concur," says Dr. Merlin.

"What now?"

"We introduce it during the Assembly," growls Jonah.

The Animal Assembly debated the Explanation for three days. It is adopted as "The Explanation of Independence of the Farms of Mt. Majesty." Almost every member of the Assembly signs it, and it was sent by Pigeon to Mr. George III, who tears it to shreds and declares the signers traitors. He puts a price on their heads.

That Explanation is read aloud throughout the whole Farm on July Fourth. Church bells ring in celebration. "We are not domesticated anymore," animals cry. "We are farmers!" The Assembly also passes a new law called the Articles of Congregation. Them Articles authorize a new independent Farm.

But the Farm still ain't got no name. Different species can't agree on one. Some say Majestic Farm. Others say Freedom Farm. In the end they call it Capitol Farm -- the Farm where animals say how their Farm is run. Capitol Farm.

Now the war wasn't goin' so good. Cold winter. Animal Army was runnin' out a' supplies. Half of enlistments soon to expire, so Cato come up with a plan. Cato's Army is pinned down in a forest valley, surrounded by men up on the heights. There's but one way out of that valley and so it's just a matter of time until the men bring their cannons along and blow them animals to smithereens. The Great Dane knows it. He's got to do somethin' and quick or he's dead.

Christmas Eve men are celebratin' 'round the campfires. Does they drink! Drinkin' songs fill the night air. Laughin' echoes over the valley. But the animals knows a secret way out. The Rapid River. Christmas Eve is so cold the Rapid freezes solid. Cato leads up the frozen river and out of that valley, campfires still burnin' down in the valley so the men thinks animals is still there. Men is toastin' George III when the Animal Army busts right into their camp! Dogs leap on drunken men who can't defend themselves. Men die. Bloody snow. Horses kick men full on the head with the hooves. Only two Dogs die. It's a rout. Ten cannon taken. Now Cato's a great general. Hearin' of Cato's victory, Pierre gives twenty cannon and a hundred men. They teach the animals to shoot. Every river guarded by Animal cannon now. Cato waits for George's men to make another mistake.

Chapter Four

They does. Late spring, George's men is trapped in a valley. Only one way out, controlled by Cato and Pierre's men. Starvin', George's men surrender to them animals. Church bells ring all over the Farm! Merlin signs the peace treaty. Mr. George III recognizes Capitol Farm!

Now you'd think life would be easy for them animals. It warn't. Each farm prints its own money. Horse Farm prints Horse dollars; Pig Farm uses pounds. Chickens take paper money; Sheep only silver coins. Goats took only gold. You see, them animals was segregated into farms according to species. Dogs and Pigs run each farm, but each farm has its own money. How do you pay for what you want to buy from another farm? No way! Trade is impossible. And there was no Capitol Farm government to do nuthin'. Them Articles of Congregation don't allow for business decisions. Each little farm is a corporation but Capitol Farm really ain't got no government to speak of.

Snapper the Fox ain't happy 'bout it. He sees Atticus. Atticus was a Hog from Pig Farm South. Friends with Scratch, who was visitin' the Pierres. He calls some big animal conference and drafts By-Laws. Animals come from all over the Farm and vote Cato president of the conference. Cato accepts, and the other animals begin debatin' business.

Now many animals don't want one big Farm. Reminds 'em of Mr. George. They wants a lot of separate small farms livin' peacable like. Chickens don't want Pigs tellin' 'em how to farm. Horses won't listen to Sheep. It's common sense. Each local farm is its own corporation. But Atticus he has a plan.

"My plan," he says to the Conference, "is something new. All smaller farms in one big corporation with a President and a Board of Directors elected by the stockholders. Each farm may form a corporation, and each stockholder may form his own corporation but the farm of each species will be a subsidiary and affiliate of Capitol Farm – the parent corporation."

"Our corporate governance must a) protect us from foreign invasion, b) protect us from wars between animals and their farms, c) procure the blessings of union between us, the smaller and the larger, the fewer and also the more numerous and d) prevent any species' farm from dominating the others."

"The Articles of Congregation have divided us – species against species. The real threat to our freedom has always been man. Humans say we cannot govern ourselves. My friends, if our system of government and business continues as heretofore, they shall prove them right! The remedy is strong centralized corporate governance."

It was a hard sell. Smaller farms refused to accept a stronger central Corporation unless they were equal to the bigger farms. In the end they agreed to split the Board of Directors into two halves as a compromise: a first part elected according to farm population, and a second part in which each species' local farm had one vote. In order to change the By-laws a majority of both parts would have to agree. Then the President would have to agree to make the change to the By-laws permanent-like.

But they still hadn't settled the issue of slavery. In the end, after a lot of talk, they compromised again. Southern farms would be allowed to import slaves for the next fifty years. Then they'd have to stop. In return northern farms would not need a two-thirds majority in the Conference to pass laws regulatin' commerce. For the purpose of the census (taken every ten years) every animal with black fur or skin was considered three-fifths of an animal. Both sides got what they wanted. Only animals not happy 'bout it was the slaves.

Them new By-Laws was sent to local farms for a vote. Atticus and Snapper wrote pamphlets supportin' ratification of course. Soon every species' farm ratified the new By-Laws, makin' Capitol Farm the parent Corporation. Then the animals elected a President per them By-laws. Cato the only choice. Nobody else ran. Made Snapper Farm Treasurer. Scratch got legal.

But even though animals won the war, Capitol Farm was still a mess. Local farms paid their soldiers with IOU's 'cause they had no money. Speculators bought IOU's from soldiers fer pennies on the dollar. Humans didn't lend money to the Farm 'cause they wanted it to fail. As Treasurer, Snapper the Fox wanted change. He thought the George family ran their farm well. He wanted a strong executive to run Capitol Farm like Mr. George so Snapper come up with a plan.

The Government of Capitol Farm would pay IOU's of Horse Farm, Dog Farm – every local farm – with IOU's from Capitol Farm. This would release local farms from all debt. Plus anybody could buy new IOU's from Capitol Farm and get a return on their money. It would all be handled by a bank – the Capitol Farm Bank.

Scratch and Atticus didn't like the plan much. They didn't want Capitol Farm run like Mr. George's farm. Scratch wanted every farm to be independent. But in a secret meetin', Snapper, Atticus and Scratch meet. The southerners agreed to Snapper's Bank if Pig Farm South became the capital of Capitol Farm. Atticus pushed the new law makin' it so through the Board of Directors, and Cato the Great Dane signed it into a new By-law. Everyone involved seemed happy but it wouldn't last.

Them speculators what bought the IOU's of the soldiers for pennies on the dollar and sold 'em to the Capitol Farm Bank for full value, they was all friends of that Fox Snapper. Pigs and Dogs, they was the only ones paid with Capitol Farm IOU's. And they was all from up North. The soldiers what got cheated in the deal, they was mostly from the South. Scratch and Atticus never forgot it. Never trusted Snapper again.

Time passes. Capitol Farm prospers but Snapper and Scratch could not agree. Animals form political parties for the first time ever. One supports the Fox; the other group, the Pig. Cato don't belong to any party. The Great Dane doesn't believe in it.

Situation comes to a crisis. Pierre's animals kill him and take his farm. Now the George family hates Pierre but they hated his animals even more. They don't want animals runnin' farms. Anywhere. And the George farm was Capitol Farm's biggest tradin' partner. So when Mr. George IV condemns the new animal revolution, Snapper does, too.

Scratch supports it and he tells the President to support it, too. Turned into a big fight between Scratch and Snapper with the Great Dane in the middle.

What does Cato do? Dog sides with the Fox. The revolution on Pierre's farm is put down. Pierre's sons take control again. Hog is so angry he quits Cato's administration and never speaks to the Great Dane or the Fox again.

Soon Cato's time as President is up. Snapper wants Cato to be President of the Corporation for life. The Great Dane refuses. After eight years Cato steps aside. Retires to private life. Best thing the big Dog ever did. For us I mean. No animal dared be an "owner" like Mr. George after that. Nobody.

Snapper wrote Cato's goin'-away speech.   The Great Dane warns against political parties on the Farm proper and human beings in general.

Urges animals be true to themselves. Retired for the rest of his life. Lot of slaves on his farm, but he freed 'em all when he dies. Last words were, "Slavery shall destroy all I have done!" Buried next to his wife on Pig Farm South. Large monument next his grave. Animals still visit it to this day.

Chapter Five

Now political parties develop all over the Farm. Cato's memory can't stop it. Some wants to grow crops. Pan-animal Party led by Scratch. Others wanted manufacturin' and minin'. Free Acreage Party. Snapper is their leader.

The next presidential elections was sour. Snapper spread rumors that Scratch mated with black Sows. But Scratch the Hog wins and becomes second President of the Corporation.

Now as author of the Explanation of Independence, Scratch believes all animals is equal. His first act as President is to make all free animals shareholders in the Corporation even if they ain't got no land. (Females and black animals ain't stockholders yet.) And Scratch sends birds explorin' and mappin' the western side of Mt. Majesty, the wilderness. They draws maps of rivers and valleys of the West, fly back and make a full report to Scratch.

The western sides of the mountain is settled by Pierre's kids. They took back the ancestral family farm from their animals, you might remember. Now they need money for a lawsuit 'gainst Mr. George IV. They sell their land to Scratch for a penny an acre. Total price $500,000.00. Capitol Farm doubles in size. Scratch gets the Board of Directors to agree, them Dogs and Pigs, and Capitol Farm is now the largest Farm in the world. Them By-Laws don't allow no new land to be added to the Farm, but the deal is too good to pass up. Scratch pays the Pierres. Besides, he says, can't risk no Georges gettin' that land.

'Cause of the new land, many animals start movin' west 'cause the corporations and banks and speculators own most of the land North and South. These animals out West wanted to join the parent Corporation of Capitol Farm. But some own slaves, some don't. Animals in the North say no slavery out West. Southerners say they can take their slaves wherever they want. In the end the President and Board of Directors agree all new farms south of the Raucous River are "slave," north of the Raucous are "free." Nobody liked the deal but it was what it was.

Meanwhile, Snapper dies in some fight. Vice President of Capitol Farm, Dog named Patches, kills the Fox. Both lived on Dog Farm North and were politically ambitious. Patches, German Shepherd, said Snapper cheated on his wife. Snapper said Patches mated with his daughter. Them was fightin' words.

Now duels was illegal. So the two lit out at night. They come to a clearin'. Snapper thinks it's a joke so he offers his neck thinkin' he'll make peace. The Dog grabs him by the throat and shakes and squeezes 'til the little Fox is done dead. He drops the body and runs off into the night.

The news hit hard. Snapper dead, too. He started the Corporation. The Fox's friends want Patches dead. He flees to the far West of Mt. Majesty. I don't rightly know what became of him. Some say he lived among the Red Deer but no one knows fer sure. Scratch the Hog says nothin' when the Fox died.

Well, you'd think them animals would a' been happy, livin' without human beings, but trouble breaks out again. Farmers in the South wanted low taxes so they could sell their crops outside the Farm. In the North animals start makin' things so they want taxes to encourage manufacturin'.

Borden, a Leghorn Rooster from Chicken Farm South wrote a pamphlet called "Nullification." Said it was the duty of southern animals to fight taxes on imports and exports. Even said the South should vote itself out of the Corporation of Capitol Farm. Lot of southerners agreed. Animals on Chicken Farm South form their own militia to secede from the Farm.

Now when President Scratch hears, the Hog is enraged. He stomps the ground and calls Borden the devil. "This will not stand," he squeals in his loudest voice, "if I have to lead the Animal Army against Chicken Farm South myself!" The President gathers the Animal Army and marches down to the border of Chicken Farm South immediately. When animals on Chicken Farm see 'emselves surrounded by Dogs and Hogs, they immediately disband their militia and make peace. Scratch is satisfied so he leads the Army back to Pig Farm South. No blood is shed – for now.

Now Capitol Farm settles down into another period of peace and prosperity. Population grows exponentially. New farms apply to join Capitol Farm. Horse Farm West and Cattle Farm West, subsidiaries, affiliates of the parent Corporation. New technologies are discovered all the time. Steam power runs mills in the North. Cotton gin allows cotton seeds to be removed by machine. Cotton production soars in the South. More slaves are needed to tend crops.

Slaves' lives are still beyond hard. Slaves had no rights. Could be skinned alive or starved, at a master's pleasure. Black-skinned animals could be sold off – to some butcher or farm owned by humans. Most masters said they lost money by ownin' slaves, but they was always tryin' get more and never free 'em. Some masters mated with their slaves, makin' their wives angry. Them children is still slaves 'cause slavery passes by the mother. Them masters, whether Dogs or Bulls or Pig or Goats, get even more slaves by fatherin' 'em themselves. Bad business!

There was a black Ram named Doug. Father, white; mother, black. Raised on Dog Farm in the South. Close to the border 'tween North and South. Livin' a few miles from freedom. His master was his father. Ram named Jenkins. Sold Doug's mom away to make his white Ewe happy. But every night the black Ewe walked ten miles to see her Lamb. After a few minutes, she turned and walked back ten miles in the dark. Her new master never knew what she was doin'.

She gets sick, dyin', Jenkins won't let Doug go and see her. She dies. Doug ain't allowed to go to her funeral. He cries when she dies. Least he still has his grandmother. Old Ewe named Mabel.

Black animals on Jenkin's farm sing in the fields. Jenkins he can't understand it. He can't bleat the same way. Doug sees black Sheep and white Sheep speak and sing differently. Different language usin' the same words.

A little older, Jenkins sends Doug to work for his brother, Ram named Ralphie. Ralphie's wife is from the North. Ewe named Molly. Molly liked Doug. Teaches Doug to read. Taught him the alphabet and simple words when Ralphie finally finds out.

"Don't you know that it is illegal to teach slaves to read!?" he bleats at her. "Do you want to get me thrown in jail?!"

"I didn't know!" bleats Molly. "Is it really 'gainst the law?"

"Course it is!" says Ralphie. "And I'm tellin' you – Molly -- fastest way to make a slave no good is teach him to read. Don't do it again!"

"I won't," says Molly. "Never again!"

So Molly wouldn't trace letters in the dirt anymore teachin' Doug to read. But the one thing he learned was that writing meant freedom. He never forgot it.

From that time on, he spends his free time learnin'. Challenges white Lambs to spellin' contests when nobody's around. Gives a white Lamb candy for definin' a word. When he's alone, he writes in the dirt and erases the letters before movin' on. He reads the family Bible when Ralphie and Molly is out. He reads their papers and letters. When he learned to read he stopped bein' a slave.

Time passes. Doug corrects Ralphie's speech one day. He says Doug is uppity and sends him back to Jenkins for breakin'. So Jenkins rents Doug to Schneider, infamous Dog for breakin' slaves. But Doug, he won't break.

Now Schneider gave his slaves enough food to eat. He just never gave 'em time to eat it. His wife lays out all kinds of food for slaves – Cattle, Horses, Goats, Sheep, even Dogs – but slaves are given only a minute to eat their fill. Then Schneider would force 'em all out of his barn and into the fields to work. An animal caught eatin' durin' work was hurt.

Schneider loved to punish slaves. He quoted the Bible when he hurt 'em. "He that knoweth his master's will and doeth it not shall be beaten with many stripes," he growls and scratches out an eye. Then laughed.

Schneider took an especial interest in Doug. Makes him a pet project. Gave him tasks the Ram had no way to complete. Then punished Doug for being disobedient. Lost part of his right ear and scar on his cheek 'cause Schneider bit him.   The Ram became scared of his own shadow. Seemed years since he read a book. And Schneider never lets up. Each day full of work. And if no work to be done, Schneider invents jobs just to keep 'em busy. One day he orders Doug to load a cart with wood, haul it and stack it. That done, Schneider then orders Doug to reload the wood, haul it back and stack it again in a different place. When Doug done that Schneider tells him to take it to a third place and stack it, and so on. By the end of the day Doug is exhausted. He can't go on. That Dog took part of an ear for that.

That night, Doug run off to hide in the woods. Schneider sees him gone and says if Doug don't come back next morning Schneider'll sic slave packs on him. Now the slave packs is roving gangs of Dogs just lookin' for runaway slaves. They's brutal. Nobody likes 'em 'cept Schneider.

Meanwhile, Doug hides in his grandma's shack in the woods. After years of service, Jenkins cut Mabel loose to die in the forest. Half-blind and old. No one would buy her. Jenkins couldn't sell her as a slave or meat.

"Son," says the old Ewe, "you got to go back. The Dogs'll kill you!"

"Reckon I'm already dead, Granma," Doug says. "All dead inside. Can't go back...."

The Ewe sipped some water and cleared her throat.

"Ain't spoke of this before, but I heard tell of a plant growin' in these here woods. If an animal eat this plant, he can't be no slave no more."

"What plant?"

"This here plant," she continues, "got the name Moley. White flower, green leaf, root as black as you n' me. I ain't never seen this plant."

She smiled.

"What do I do with it?"

"Ya eat it – flower, leaf n' root! Makes you strong, they says, so strong you can't be slave no more."

"Go back, son! Find this plant, then go back."

"Alright. I'll find me some Moley," the Ram says. "Then back."

So Doug goes lookin' for Moley. He seen plants with white flowers, but they got white roots. Never seen no plant with white flowers and black roots. He searches late in the night, diggin' up every white-flowered plant he can find. Every one has white roots. Then the moon comes out from behind a cloud, and there it stands. He sees it: white flowers shaped like shootin' stars. Without thinkin' he digs at the roots. They was black! He washes the plant in a stream and swallows it -- flowers, leaves and the roots. Then he lays down on the ground and falls asleep.

Next day, Schneider sees Doug go in his slave shack, so Schneider comes out of his barn and walks over to Doug's shack.

"Come out here, you goddam Lamb!" Schneider yells. "Come out and take yer punishment!" (Masters call black Rams "Lambs" to humiliate 'em.)

Doug steps out to face Schneider. Locks eyes with the mongrel and charges. Horns strike Schneider in his chest, pushin' him backwards. Dog falls down in the dirt, hittin' a rock with his head. Springs to his feet again but Schneider don't know what to do. No slave ever hit him before. He don't like it. It was against the law. Penalty -- death, so Schneider cannot believe it. And everyone is watchin' now.

"I'll show you who's boss!" Dog growls, leapin' at Doug's throat, but Doug is too quick for him. Hits Schneider, knocks out some of his teeth. Schneider spits 'em out on the ground.

The whole farm is watchin' the fight. Doug sees 'em standin' round in a circle. Schneider's spittin' blood on the dirt and coughin'.

Now Dog barks as loud as he can at Doug but he's in pain. The Ram just stands watchin'. Schneider tries everythin' he can but it don't work. He lunges and jumps, feints and rolls. Each time Doug's horns hit him.

"Well, I've taught you your lesson!" Schneider finally gasps. "Go to work in the fields! All of you!" he barks at the slaves. Then he limps back to his barn, coughin' blood the whole way.

Doug stands there for a minute. No scratch on him, ear still bleedin' where Schneider bit him yesterday. Then he turns and walked out to work in the fields for the day.

"I'm free," he says to himself. "I'm runnin' away soon as it's right."

Doug's grandmother dies. Ain't nothin' to keep him there now. He forges a letter and waits for the day when the mongrel's away. Passes them checkpoints and sneaks into the North. Nobody suspects a black Ram with a letter. He kneels down and kisses the free soil. Then he walks up the mountain. Sprinkles his hooves with cayenne pepper to throw off the slave packs. It hurts his feet but he don't care. He follows the North Star and travels at night. Other animals help him on his way, some white ones.

But when he tries to make a livin' among whites, Doug learns he ain't welcome. Most northern whites hates slavery but they didn't love black animals neither. They hate slavery 'cause it threatens their jobs. They didn't want no black animals competin' with 'em for jobs. So nobody hires Doug. No work. Luckily he's hired by northern abolitionists to make speeches 'cause he was good at it. He even writes an autobiography, which is a big hit on the George family farm. Them Georges loves to say animals on Capitol Farm is hypocrites fer talkin' freedom but ownin' slaves.

Chapter Six

New farms spring up out West. Mostly free. Slave owners in the South don't like it. Say they's bein' surrounded. 'Fraid the Board of Directors'll outlaw slavery. So they goes west and takes slaves with 'em. Events now took place that leads to war 'tween North and the South over slavery.

The Corporation's Board of Directors changed the By-laws. New farms joinin' Capitol Farm choose to be slave or free. Seein' a chance, pro-slavery and anti-slavery animals invade them new territories, hopin' to make farms slave or free. Goat Farm West: fightin' turns bloody. Bulldog named Comet kills four pro-slavery Terriers. Crushes their windpipes. Then moves to Pig Farm South. With runaway slaves and some abolitionists, he takes the Sheriff's barn on Pig Farm. They kill a Great Dane – Cato's grand nephew. Hopes local slaves'll join him in revolt. Never happens. Dog named Hannibal leads a pack of soldiers to put down the revolt. Comet is tried and executed for treason 'gainst Pig Farm. His last words are, "The sin of slavery will not be washed away except by blood!" He hangs.

A lot of animals said Comet was a terrorist. Northern animals, some said he was right. Now Abel spoke out against Comet. He was a lanky Horse from Horse Farm West. Opposed the spread of slavery to new farms. Thought black animals was inferior to whites, but he says Comet was wrong. Abel was a lawyer. He campaigned for a seat on the Board of Directors 'gainst a big fat Hog named Tiny. Tiny was the incumbent and a pillar of the Pananimal Party. Abel opposed him because Tiny voted to allow slavery on new farms out west. The debates between 'em focused the Farm on the question of slavery. Debates was held throughout the Farm but began on Cattle Farm West.

"I remember many years ago," Tiny began, "when I was but a young Pig. At that time, my good friend Abel and I had one thing in common. We were struggling lawyers here on Cattle Farm West. He joined the Free Acreage Party, while I joined the Pananimal Party, which is the party of President Scratch. Now we find ourselves contending for the same seat on the Board of Directors."

"I have three questions for my friend. First, is he against the admission of new farms into the Corporation if the animals on those farms vote to allow slavery? Second, does he support the ruling of the Capitol Farm Court in the Jennings case? Third, does he wish to grant black animals social equality with white animals? Would he have us marry blacks?"

"I ask this so that when I trot my good friend Abel through the Farm he may not say different things to please animals on different farms. My position is one and the same in the North and in the South and has been known for many years!" [Applause.]

At first Abel looked his audience up and down from the dais where he stood in the flickerin' torchlight. His voice was reedy. Unusual fer a big Horse.

"My good friend, Tiny, is under a misapprehension. Those were not three questions which he asked. They were four!" [Laughs from the crowd.]

"Let me answer my friend's four questions. First, I do not oppose the admission of new slave farms to the Corporation if animals on those farms genuinely vote to allow slavery on those farms. Second, I do not support the ruling of the Capitol Farm Court in the Jennings case. The ruling was wrong because it nullifies our right to prohibit slavery here on Cattle Farm West. That is a subversion of our government. The Jennings ruling must be overturned!" [Cheers.]

"As to Tiny's third and fourth questions – I do not believe black and white animals are equals, nor do I think different colored animals ought to mix."

"The question we must ask ourselves is this: is slavery as an institution good or bad?   Then we must ask ourselves: Does it enrich and strengthen the Corporation – or does it diminish it?"

"Tiny says he doesn't care if new farms are slave or free. These are the words of one who does not see slavery as an evil. Tiny ignores slavery's moral nature."

"We see here the confrontation of two principles. The first says, 'You do the work and earn the food, and I will eat it.' It is the practice of human beings like the Georges who have enslaved animals for thousands of years. The second is the common right of all animals – stated in the Explanation of Independence, that 'All animals are created equal and are endowed by their Creator with certain inalienable rights, that among these are life, liberty and the pursuit of happiness.' I tell you, in respect of these rights, black animals are my equal and yours." [Applaudin'.]

"As to my second question, is it not clear that slavery has always been a cause of disharmony among us?   [Applaudin'.]   If the current situation continues, will not our children and our children's children be divided by the question of slavery? I say to you, 'A house divided against itself cannot stand.' I believe this Corporation cannot endure half-slave and half-free. I do not expect the Corporation to be dissolved. I do not expect the house to fail – but I do expect it will cease to be divided. It will become all slave or all free."

"Tiny and his friends seem now to support the perpetuation and nationalization of slavery. We in the Free Acreage Party seek its end."

"I am a Horse who from humble beginnings have labored to improve himself. I am the first Horse to ever run for a seat on the Board of Directors.

Like many of you, I pulled a plow and can work for myself. I hauled loads for another animal. I scrimped and saved to study so I could become my own boss. I believe that labor is prior to and independent of capital; that in fact capital is the fruit of labor, and could never have existed if labor had not existed first. I hold that labor is the superior – greatly the superior – of capital. And chief among all our labors is education. To some, education of laborers is not only useless but pernicious and dangerous. But free labor says, 'No!' It argues that the Author of every animal gave a teachable mind and an able body to each. No community whose every member possesses an education can ever be the victim of oppression in any of its forms. Such community will be alike independent of crowned-kings, money-kings and land-kings."

Tiny defeats Abel in a landslide. But owin' to his speeches, Abel the Horse is leader of the Free Acreage Party. First animal not a Dog or a Pig to run for President of the Corporation.

Next year Corporation holds an election for President. Abel's clear choice of the Free Acreage Party 'cause he hates slavery. Pananimals are split down the middle. In the North they wants Tiny as President, but them southerners want some Ram name of Holling. Abel doesn't get a majority of votes in the election but because them Pananimals is divided, Abel gets elected.

The South mourns. Southern animals is convinced Abel's gonna abolish slavery. Chicken Farm South secedes from the Corporation. Then Sheep Farm, Goat Farm, Dog Farm, Horse Farm and Goose Farm. Pig Farm can't decide. Chumling, a Yorkshire Boar now President of Capitol Farm 'til Abel gets sworn in, does nothin'. Finally, Pig Farm goes too. The Rebels declare themselves a new Farm called the Congregation of the Farms on Mt. Majesty – "Congregation" for short. They say they's a voluntary organization like a church. Hence the name: Congregation – where member farms can come and go as they please. Unlike the Corporation where you is locked in. They pick a President, Holling the Hog. He asks the Georges and the Pierres for guns and money.

Now even though they did most of the fightin' and dyin' in the war, free soldiers in the South ain't got no slaves. Rich animals' war; poor animals' fight, they says. Common animals don't vote to secede from the Corporation, neither. Rich plantation owners vote to secede. But whites in the South hoped to own slaves someday so they went along with it. Most whites support the Rebellion and joins local militias.

Abel can't do nothin' 'bout secession 'til he's President. He makes speeches in the North as he travels to Pig Farm South. In Pig Farm North he says to supporters:

"I am filled with deep emotion, finding myself standing here where were collected together the wisdom, the patriotism, the devotion to principle, from which sprang the institutions under which we live. You have kindly suggested to me that in my power is the task of restoring peace to our distracted farmland. I can say in return that I have never had a feeling politically that did not spring from the Explanation of Independence."

"I have often inquired of myself, what great principle or idea it was that has kept Capitol Farm so long together. It was not the mere separation from the George family farm; but something in that Explanation giving liberty not only to the animals of this Farm, but hope to the world for all future time. It was that which gave promise that in due time the weights should be lifted from the shoulders of all animals, and that *all* should have an equal chance.   This is the sentiment embodied in the Explanation of Independence."

"If this farmland cannot be saved without giving up that principle, I would rather be assassinated on this spot than to surrender it."

"In the present circumstances, there is no need of bloodshed and war. Let me say in advance, there will be no bloodshed unless it be forced upon the Corporation. The Corporation will not use force unless force is used against it. I have no purpose, directly or indirectly, to interfere with the institution of slavery on the farms where it exists. I believe I have no lawful right to do so, and I have no inclination to do so."

"My friends, this is a wholly unprepared speech. I did not expect to be called upon to say a word when I came here. I may, therefore, have said something indiscreet, but I have said nothing but what I am willing to live by, and, in the pleasure of Almighty God, die by."

Then friends discover a plot by southerners to kill Abel before he can become President of Capitol Farm. He changes his schedule, disguises himself as a Pack Mule and slips quietly into Pig Farm South one mornin' before dawn. Abel spent the days before his swearin' in in hidin' but when he became President he says the followin' words to the South.

"In your power, my dissatisfied fellow animals, and not in mine, is the momentous issue of Civil War. The government will not assail you. You can have no conflict without being the aggressors. You have no oath registered in heaven to destroy the Corporation, while I shall have the most solemn one to 'preserve, protect and defend' it."

"I am loath to close. We are not enemies, but friends. We must not be enemies. Though passion may have strained, it must not break our bonds of affection. The mystic chords of memory, stretching from every battlefield, and patriot grave, to every living heart and hearthstone, all over this broad land, will yet swell the chorus of Capitol Farm when again touched, as they surely will be, by the better angels of our nature."

Nothin' happened. North and South eye each other from armed camps; no shots fired; no blood shed.

On an island in the middle of the Raucous River a-runnin' through Chicken Farm South stands Fort Henry. Made out of stone and owned by the Corporation. Animals on Chicken Farm refuse to sell supplies to Fort Henry so Major Braddock, the commandin' officer, writes Abel askin' what to do. Should he take what he needs by force or wait? Meanwhiles, Rebels surround the fort with cannons demandin' Braddock's surrender. The whole mountain is watchin' the standoff.

After a week, the Rebels begin to fire, lightnin' up the sky. Shelling for twelve hours. Finally Braddock waves the white flag. Animal Civil War is begun.

The North, triple population of the South, readies for war. Abel calls fer enlistments. Young 'uns join the Animal Army. War'll last three weeks, they say. Northern fact'ries put out cannon and guns like never before.

Then President Abel appoints a Giant Schnauzer called Scout to head the Animal Army, which now takes up defensive positions 'round the Farm's capital, place called Pig Rocks in northern Pig Farm South. Scout drills new recruits as they pours down the mountain from northern farms. Each is given a blue cap and a satchel of provisions. Rifles is given to teams of animals. One aims and fires; the other holds 'er steady. Bang! Bang, bang! Pigs and Dogs make up most of the infantry. Pigs can pull triggers with their knuckles. Oxen and Horse pulled cannon. Them Birds are spies.

Abel made sure the animals what surrendered at Fort Henry is released. Had 'em to dinner at the President's barn, then starts studyin' military theory.

Chapter Seven

Havin' made the Animal Army a grand fightin' machine, Scout the Schnauzer sits on his ass and does nothin'. Didn't attack. Didn't do nothin'. 'Cept defend capital of the Farm place called Pig Rocks named after these boulders that looked like Hogs. The South's Army, Army of the Congregation, took up defensive positions round about Pig Falls. Pig Falls was capital of the Congregation also on Pig Farm South.

Now Abel's strategy was to isolate the South, keep it from sellin' crops to Mr. George and Pierre. Scout the Giant Schnauzer says (President Abel believed him) he can defeat the South just by takin' Pig Falls. Meanwhiles, Abel's generals in the West could take the Ramblin' River – and so cut the Congregation in two from North to South. (The Ramblin' deserved its name.) Then those generals come east and take Pig Falls and the Congregation's over. That's the Horse's plan.

But Scout don't want to attack. Says Abel don't know nothin' 'bout war 'cause Abel's a Horse not a Dog. Every day the Congregation grows stronger, and the odds that the Georges or Pierres'll help the South increased. Oh yeah -- and the enlistment of soldiers in the Animal Army is set to expire. Abel orders Scout to attack now, which the Schnauzer does at Bantam Heights. On a perfect July mornin', birds singin' in the trees, Corporation troops march down the mountainside to Bantam Heights. Animal Army outnumbers the Congregationalists two to one, but them northern animals ain't disciplined. Takes 'em two full days when it should have only taken one. And then, when he gets there, Scout doesn't attack, even though he outnumbers them Rebels.

Commander of South's army is Hannibal, a Beagle. He knows how to fight. Hannibal brings up reinforcements while Scout waits. Now the armies is equal.

Each army attacks other's left flank. Rebel lines hold until Bulls from Cattle Farm West charge 'em. But them Bulls only reach Bantam Heights where a Hog named Christian and his soldiers stand like a stone wall. These Pigs is crack shots. They got guts. The Bulls go down in blood and smoke and iron. They don't get up out of that dust. Northerners behind 'em is slaughtered. The Animal Army's center breaks. Hannibal takes their cannon. Animal Army runs for its life droppin' rifles and supplies behind 'em all the way to Pig Rocks.

Defeat embarrasses the Giant Schnauzer. Abel asks why he lost. Scout says he needs more soldiers. Fresh troops are provided, but Scout does nothin' with 'em for the next six weeks. Finally Abel visits Scout in camp and orders him to attack again.

Next battle to the southeast of Pig Falls. Scout'll cross the Rowdy River on pontoons, sneak up on Pig Falls and force Hannibal to give up. If not, cannon'll lay waste to Pig Falls.

When the Animal Army reaches the Rowdy there's nobody there. But pontoons ain't been brought down yet. By the time the pontoons arrive it's too late. Hannibal's army holds the other shore. Dogs and Pigs with guns. Rebels is shielded by a stone wall. They fire down at northerners comin' up from the Rowdy River. Fourteen times Scout orders the Animal Army to charge a stone wall. Every time it fails. Five thousand die chargin' the wall. Finally Scout gives up, tail between his legs. He takes up a defensive position again around Pig Rocks.

Meanwhiles, out west, a rumpled old Bulldog is successful. General Scruff takes the Ramblin' River and cuts the South in two. He drinks and cusses and smokes cigars and plays poker. Abel don't care. He fires Scout and gives Scruff command.

Now that Beagle Hannibal was confident 'cause of winnin' at the Rowdy River. He decides to invade the North. Victory on northern soil will bring the George family into the war, he says. Plus his soldiers need supplies. Easiest place to get 'em is the North. Invades Pig Farm North, place called the Hub. Largest battle ever on Capitol Farm's soil.   (Local animals called it the Hub 'cause four roads meet there.)

Southern Horses needed horseshoes, so they wandered to the Hub. Northern cavalry met the Rebels in the Hub's center. Fierce battle ensues. Neither side able to gain advantage. Horses died. Come nightfall each side retreated and sent for reinforcements.

Dogs, Goats, Hogs, Rams and Bulls come to the Hub. North seizes hills overlookin' the town. Hannibal orders general named Wharton, a Boxer, to take the Hillock. But Wharton delayed his attack.   After three hours, Scruff the Bulldog arrives with reinforcements. That was the first day. North held the Hillock. More reinforcements come for South and North.

On the second day of fightin', Hannibal again orders Wharton to take the Hillock.

"I do not want to attack the Hillock, Sir," he says to Hannibal. "Why not pivot eastward toward Pig Rocks so as to draw enemy forces onto level ground?"

The Beagle was irate. "I have chosen to fight here!" he barks. "Now follow your orders or relinquish your command!"

The Dog orders to attack. Rebel Dogs, Horses, Rams and Bulls charge. Hogs support 'em with cannon fire and their muskets. Them soldiers is almost to the top of the Hillock when Corporation Bulls, Rams and Dogs come runnin' 'cross the face of the hill. Wharton's soldiers is blind-sided.

They drop their guns and run. Northern Pigs shoot down most of 'em. Rollin' down the hill to die in the dust.

On the third day, Hannibal chooses a frontal assault 'gainst the northern line stretchin' 'tween the Hillock and Hub Heights. Southern artillery shells the Animal Army early. Northern soldiers is killed sleepin' in tents or eatin' breakfast. But Scruff answers shot for shot, fire for fire, then all silent. Hannibal thinks Scruff is out of ammo so he charges 'cross a wheat field up at northern lines. But the North ain't out of ammo. It's a trick. When Rebels had almost reached the northern line, Scruff gives the order to fire. Wherever that Animal Army shot Reb's fall. Ten at a shot. Northern Hogs and Dogs aim from behind a stone wall and rake the Rebels with fire. The Congregation was all blood and dust and smoke and flyin' dirt as they fall. It was a slaughter. Six thousand Rebel soldiers die in the charge alone. South lost the War that day. Hannibal's army would never be the same.

Greetin' his soldiers as they retreated from the Hub, the Beagle wept. "It is my fault, all my fault," the Dog says as he walked south to Pig Falls.

Battle of the Hub was the largest of the Animal Civil War. 7,300 Rebels died. 2,800 Corporation soldiers died. All buried there at the Hub.

Two months later, President Abel made the battlefield a cemetery. Memorial to the fallen. He says at the dedication:

"Thirty-seven years ago, our fathers brought forth a new Farm upon this mountain, conceived in liberty, and dedicated to the proposition that all animals are created equal."

"Now we are engaged in a great Civil War, testing whether that Farm, or any farm so conceived and so dedicated, can long endure. We are met on a great battlefield of that War. We have come to dedicate a portion of that field, as a final resting place for those who here gave their lives that that Farm might live. It is altogether fitting and proper that we should do this."

"But in a larger sense, we can not dedicate – we can not consecrate – this ground. The brave animals, living and dead, who struggled here, have consecrated it, far above our poor power to add or detract. The world will little note, nor long remember what we say here, but it can never forget what they did here. It is for us the living, rather, to be dedicated here to the unfinished work which they who fought here have thus far so nobly advanced. It is rather for us to be here dedicated to the great task remaining before us – that from these honored dead we take increased devotion to that cause for which they gave the last full measure of devotion – that we here highly resolve that these dead shall not have died in vain – that this farmland, under God, shall have a new birth of freedom – and that government of animals, by animals, for animals, shall not perish from the earth."

Week later, as commander-in-chief of Capitol Farm's armed forces, Abel issued the Emancipation Justification in which he freed slaves in servitude on Rebel farms.

"And I further declare and make known, that such animals of suitable condition, will be received into the armed service of Capitol Farm to garrison forts, positions, stations and other places, and to maintain vessels of all sorts in said service."

Black animals, includin' Doug escaped to the North, is overjoyed. They floods the Animal Army. Accepted by some whites. But many northerners is still prejudiced. Yet now Scruff got the superior numbers to take Pig Falls.

Meanwhile, Scruff's friend General Mephisto, cigar-smokin' Boxer, drives east from the Ramblin' River, cuttin' the South in two yet again. Mephisto burns and destroys every barn and shed in his path. His troops kill crops and cut down trees in and out of their path. When he reaches the village of Olympus on Horse Farm South, he burns it to the ground.

"War is hell," the Boxer explains. "I will do whatever it takes to end this one!" Then he drives east all the way to the Rancid River and turns north to take Hannibal from behind.

When news of Mephisto burnin' Olympus reaches the North there's jubilation. Abel wins the next presidential election 'cause of Mephisto. Scout the Schnauzer is nominated by the Pananimals on a peace platform, and it looked like Abel is gonna lose, but Mephisto's march changes all that.

Meanwhile, caught between Scruff and Mephisto, Hannibal sees he ain't gonna win. Hannibal surrenders to Scruff to save his troops, endin' the Animal Civil War, bloodiest war in Farm history.

Abel urges mercy toward the Congregation. Three days later he attends theater in Pig Rocks. Watchin' the show, he is shot in the head by a Pig callin' himself Brutus but whose given name is Kane. The Horse dies. No one can save him. The theater crowd, seein' what happens, kills Kane on the spot and dumps his body in the river.

Abel's funeral procession wends its way back to Cattle Farm West. Churches ring bells. Animals stop to pay respects to the Horse who held the Corporation together. A poet called Whitey, platinum Golden Retriever from Dog Farm North, writes these lines about Abel:

O Captain! my Captain! our fearful trip is done;
The ship has weather'd every rack, the prize we sought is won,
The port is near, the bells I hear, the people all exulting
While follow eyes the steady keel, the vessel grim and daring:

But O heart! heart! heart!
O the bleeding drops of red,
Where on the deck my Captain lies,
Fallen cold and dead.

Abel's still buried on Horse Farm West. Many animals think he's the best President the Corporation ever had.

Chapter Eight

The Corporation was hard on the South. You know, occupied by troops. Forced into takin' loyalty oaths. Readmitted to the Farm afterwards.

Black animals was now citizens. They could vote and run for office. Blacks was even elected to the Board of Directors. But their freedom was fleetin'. Southern farms passed new laws 'gainst black animals. Like where they could live, what they did fer a livin' and what schoolin' they could get. And then there's unwritten laws. Color rules. It was against the law fer a white Horse to marry a black Horse, and so on.

And if 'n a black animal was convicted of a crime, he works for nothin' in prison. So whites make more money from black animal convicts than they did off them slaves to begin with. Black convicts loses the right to vote -- fer life. Blacks is still slaves 'cept in name. In name they're free. So they up and leave the South and walked up the mountainside to northern farms. Northern farms are big towns now. Commerce. Industry. The poor livin' in small coops and pens. They don't own land no more. Wealthy animals had all the big barns, clean water and fresh air.

Now the North's business community growed and growed. Manufacturin' powerhouses. Companies all over. Soon they's exportin' goods all over the world. Clothin', minerals, and oil. Human beings want animal products 'cause they's cheap.

Then the High Court of Capitol Farm decides that the Explanation of Independence and the Emancipation Justification don't apply mainly to real animals. Instead, they applies 'em to corporations. A corporation is an animal, Court says. Now the Court don't specify if a corporation is a Hog or a Dog or even a Goat. But because the Court says it, animals most believe it: Corporations is animals, legally speakin'.

And since the Free Acreage Party controls them Board of Directors, wealthy northerners on the Board changes the Corporation's name from "Capitol Farm" to "Capital Farm." "The real purpose of the Farm is to provide a return to those investing money," they says. "Not for animals to vote. Most animals won't notice the difference in names anyway." And they was right. The names sounded the same, and most animals didn't even know what them words mean. So public signs is changed from "Capitol Farm" to "Capital Farm" everywhere. And nobody notices. So the wealth, the land of Capital Farm is owned by a few families of animals.

Thing is, they gets greedy. 'Stead of being happy just making a livin', they wants its all. I'm talkin' monopoly. They starts off capitalists but transmutates into monopolists what own everythin'. Monopolists is a different kind of animal from you and me. They's monopolists in capitalist clothin', you know, like Wolves in Sheep's clothin' -- somethin' outta Aesop and the Bible. Ain't nothin' new. But they lose their love for a free market. They wants monopoly not freedom. 'Cept when the Corporation starts to regulate 'em. Then they cries for free markets again until they can start their monopolies.

There was a Greyhound name of Rocky what cornered the market in kerosene. He pays the Corporation $300.00 so he don't have to fight in the Civil War like poor animals. (Rich animals always gets out of fightin' that way.) Now Rocky never smiles or laughs. Never goes out drinkin' or gamblin' or nothin'. Religious Dog. Northern Baptist. Had but one vice. Dog loved money. More than his own soul. Makes a fortune sellin' crappy rifles to Animal Army durin' the Civil War. (Gun explodes. Kills the soldier dead.) Takes the money and puts it in oil. Background's in accountin', but he buys every oil refinery on Capital Farm and creates a monopoly, what he calls "an ark of salvation."

"I am an angel of mercy," Rocky growls. "Sent by the Lord to bring order to this ungodly chaos." Starts by buyin' oil refineries on Pig Farm North. Cut secret deals fer barges and bridges. Capital Farm is crisscrossed by rivers. To connect 'em, animals dug canals. Quickest way to ship goods. Rocky makes barge owners give him a discount for shippin' oil, rebate fer competitor's oil they move. Keeps politicians happy by payin' 'em off. Soon Rocky owns all the refineries on Capital Farm, every one. One lone Dog settin' the price for kerosene round the whole planet.

"Another refinery in the fold!" he barks. Buyin' out somebody he ruins. Richest animal in the world. Richer than God, some say.

"Money is poetry," he says. Lives in a modest barn. 'Stead of givin' money to his Pups, makes 'em do chores for cash. Dog loved spirituals. Loved to visit black churches. Gave money to college for black Ewes on Sheep Farm South. "God chose me to be rich. My wealth is sign of divine favor," he says to them Sheep at commencement. "Every rich animal has been predestined to go to heaven. That's God's will. That is the Gospel of Wealth." Most animals believe Rocky's Gospel of Wealth. Blamed themselves for bein' poor even if they worked hard and got nuthin'. Think God's judgin' 'em.

Same time, the conservation movement begins on Capital Farm. Mountain Goat named Johnny settles the western reaches of Mt. Majesty and starts writin' books about the land. Wants to redeem it from pollution. "Nature's cathedral" he calls it. The President was a pink Hog named Rosy at that time. Wore pince-nez spectacles and traveled to Capital Farm West. Camped out with Johnny under the redwoods hundreds of feet high, more than three thousand years old.

"I don't open the Bible if I want to see God," Johnny tells the President. "I go out into the wild."

"I will sit down all day to make the acquaintance of a plant or flower. I ask the boulders where they hail from – and where they are going. I listen to the songs of waterfall and thunderstorm."

"Sometimes at night I shout down into the canyon from where I am sleeping. It's so deep that I am awakened the next morning by my echo."

"What would you have me do?" says the President, firelight-in' on his specs.

"Do you see this natural beauty, the closest thing we have to Eden?"

"Yes, I do."

"Leave it alone. You cannot improve upon it. Nature's bounty will flow into animals on the Farm like sunshine into trees for countless generations. Your children, your children's children, will bless your name after you are gone. When you go into the wild, you are going home. Don't destroy your home!"

President listened to Johnny. Beginning on Capital Farm West, he makes national parks belongin' to all the animals on the Farm, black and white, rich and poor, immigrant and native born. First national parks in world history. They still exist today.

"Our greatest national heritage," said Rosy in a speech, "is nature itself."

But even if the parks was free, most animals ain't got time to enjoy 'em. Most work long days in fields and factories. Six days a week. Their lives is drudgery and squalor. Their employers gots easy lives. Enjoyin' the beauty of Mt. Majesty. Seein' such inequality, educated animals begin to organize workin' animals into unions. One organizer's an Irish Moiled Cow named Mother Nan.

"Poverty," she moos, "is a crime perpetrated by the rich against the poor. It is a crime condoned by our churches, our schools, our newspapers and our courts. All of our laws are directed against the working animal. 'But this is a Dog-eat-Dog world,' monopolist animals say. And they use their money to buy our churches, our schools, our newspapers and our courts."

"But I say to you animals, laissez-faire capitalism is laissez-faire cannibalism. Dog eat Dog! Monopoly. Jehovah, the God of battles, and my voice will stop these idolators from grinding the face of the poor!"

"Remember: Whatever we animals may not have, we have free speech, and no one can take that away from us!"

Crowd of workin' animals cheered this speech, but the Dog Farm police charged the podium where she stands. Shut down the meetin' and arrested the Cow as an anarchist. Jailed her for two weeks. Chief of police scratches out her right eye with his claws.

She don't give up. Mother Nan redoubles her efforts for the poor. Marches with Lambs, Calves, Foals, Kids and Puppies to President Rosy's home on Dog Farm North. Them children lost eyes, ears, noses, lips and limbs on the job. Mother Nan brings 'em to the President's barn to show him the evils of child labor. Rosy won't see 'em but the march is a success.

But a depression hits the Farm. Many animals ain't got nothin' to eat. Mother Nan tells the starvin' to go to them farms of the rich to take food. Police hear what she says and jailed her for two years fer incitin' riots. Mother Nan preaches her "gospel" to everyone in prison anyway, and when she's released she throws herself once again into the animal labor movement. By this time many animals out West lost their farms to banks. If sale of a farm didn't pay the mortgage, animals was sold off as food to humans or eaten by bank executives.

Now Rocky owns a coal mine out on Goat Farm West. Miners go on strike fer wages. Rocky brings in immigrants to dig coal and strikers take possession of the mines, refusin' to let "scabs" work. Governor of Goat Farm calls in the local militia paid by Rocky. It's a standoff. Strikers livin' in tents through the winter and militia camped above 'em on the hills.

When the strikers doesn't go, Rocky tells the governor he has to do somethin'. Invites strike's leader, Italian Mule named Enzo, to parley. When Enzo shows up to the meetin' he's killed and then eaten by them Dogs in the militia. Now the Hogs in the militia begin firin' into the strikers' camp. Females and the young 'uns is killed. Then the militia sets fire to the tents. But lots of females and youngsters is dug in 'neath them tents to 'scape the bullets. They burn to death. Smell of burnin' flesh fills the air.

News of the massacre quickly spreads. Barge workers refuse to transport soldiers to the mine. Members of local militia join the strikers.

After holdin' funerals, miners strike back. They blows up mine shafts with dynamite and seize the governor's barn. He flees up Mt. Majesty. President Rosy sends in the Animal Army. The strike is put down. Strike leaders is convicted and eaten by judge and jury of local Dogs. Mother Nan's life is spared 'cause she's female but she's banned from Goat Farm West for the rest of her life.

Now local farms and the Corporation begins to crack down on unions through Capital Farm. Convictin' organizers of bein' anarchists, socialists and communists.

Makin' matters worse, animals on a Farm near the George family farm rebel and take over a farm from their owners. Commie Farm. They practices communism and doesn't use money, or so they says. Birds bring news of that new farm. Politicians like Rosy use "godless communism" as an excuse to arrest animals on Capital Farm.

Chapter Nine

More authorities crack down on labor unions, more they grow. Worse things got fer workin' animals, more they want to succeed. They got thrown in jail, lost their jobs. Some eaten by police. To make workers happy, President Rosy and the Board of Directors changes them By-Laws to limit monopoly. (Secretly Rosy tells business leaders he ain't gonna enforce them new laws. Says its "good business" appeasin' workers 'cause it prevents commies and socialists from complainin'.) Rosy also wants health insurance for the whole Farm, but the Board don't. Nothin' happens on that.

The common animal's situation changes when Capital Farm declares war on Mr. Wilhelm. Wilhelm lives east of the George family farm. George asks animals to fight on his side, but them animals is neutral at first. "It's a fight between human beings," animals say. "We animals should stay out of it!"

After Wilhelm's men grab the Farm's wagons takin' crops to George, Rosy asks the Board fer war 'gainst Mr. Wilhelm. The Board grants Rosy war powers, so now animals is fightin' 'longside George's and Pierre's men. (Later it got known that them seized wagons was carryin' rifles and cannon made by them animals fer them Georges, but by then war's over.)

To maintain order, Rosy and the Board pass their Anti-Spy By-Law. Still law today. If you says anything negative 'bout Capital Farm, they can lock you up. But 'stead of goin' after spies, they use the law to break them unions since workers is critical of the war.

Now a Mallard called Plato was head of the Capital Farm Socialist Party. He starts out workin' on bridges and barges out west. One day the Duck converts to Socialism cause his brother dies on the job. Hell, he even ran for President couple times. Each time he gets more votes than before. The Corporation follows him around and considers Plato a threat.

"This country cannot be half slave and half free," Plato quacks one day quotin' President Abel. Out on Cattle Farm West. "Economically, we working animals are slaves. Yet the labor movement means more than a paltry increase in wages. Our aim is to abolish the system of wage slavery and achieve the freedom of the entire working class, in fact, the freedom of the entire animal population. That is my gospel. I will preach this gospel until the Good Lord takes me!"

"You know that I have no love for Mr. Wilhelm. But I see no reason why young Bulls, Dogs, Horses, Hogs and Sheep should fight for human beings! Why would an animal ever fight for *men*? What have human beings ever done for animals? They have mistreated us, enslaved us for centuries."

"Our politicians tell us we live in a free republic; that our institutions serve every animal; that all animals are free because we govern ourselves without human interference. That's too much, even for a joke!"

"Wars have always been fought for conquest and plunder. The master class declares the wars to make money. The underclass fights the wars."

"Now the Corporation is drafting young animals into its Animal Army. I encourage all youngsters to refuse to fight this war of empire and plunder. I encourage them to have sympathy, as I do, for every living thing." He pauses while the crowd listens.

"The day will come when socialists will sweep into power on this Farm and throughout the world. We will destroy enslaving capitalist institutions and recreate them in our own image. The sun of capitalism is setting. The sun of socialism is rising!"

The crowd cheers his speech but next day Plato is arrested for bein' a spy. At trial the Duck won't make no defense nor call no witnesses. Denies none of the charges and speaks only at sentencin'.

"Your honor, years ago I recognized my kinship with all living beings, and I made up my mind that I was not one bit better than the meanest on earth. I said then, as I say now, that while there is a lower class, I am in it; while there is a criminal element, I am of it; while there is a soul in prison, I am not free."

Hog named Boris sentenced him to be killed and eaten by police, after the jury found him guilty of spyin'. Only Dogs and Pigs is on that jury. Execution of Plato unleashes a wave of violence 'gainst socialists and labor unions. Newspapers call 'em traitors. Collaborators with Wilhelm. Capital Farm's Socialist Party died with Plato.

Them Allies won the war. Strict sanctions 'gainst Mr. Wilhelm. Rosy wants freedom fer animals on Wilhelm's farm. George and Pierre says no. Them animals ain't free. Sanctions 'gainst Wilhelm was vindictive as hell. His animals had nothin' to eat. They starve.

But it was good times on Capital Farm again. Gap 'tween rich and poor was there, but animals enjoyed a high standard of livin'. Tough time on Wilhelm's farm. No food.

War made a lot of money for Rocky and his friends. Sold oil, guns, food, cotton, machines to George and Pierre. Unions busted. Cash-rich rich. There warn't no regulation of business. No limit to the money to be made.

Rocky starts buyin' up banks 'cause animals wants to borrow money. Farm land is expensive. Speculators snatch it up. Manufacturers keep makin' stuff but they can't sell it. Market's flooded with stuff no animals want. And businesses got two sets of books – one for the Corporation and one fer investors. Nobody knows what a company's really worth. Nobody cares. Lotta easy money.

Day of recknin' come at last when drought hits the Farm. Farmers and speculators default. Banks default on loans from other banks. Banks made loans one hundred times their reserves. Defaults start a "domino effect" causin' half Capital Farm's banks to go bankrupt. Open banks stop lendin' and call in their loans. But nobody can pay 'em back. Without no money, businesses can't pay their employees, so they lay them off. Thirty percent of animals is unemployed. And they can't buy nothin' without no jobs, so they gets evicted from their barns.

Unemployed animals wander farm streets lookin' for work. There was actually plenty to eat, but the unemployed could not afford to buy. Many farmers dumped crops in the rivers to keep the price from droppin' – as hungry animals helplessly watched the waste, starvin'.

"The problem," Rocky says in a newspaper interview, "is too much regulation."

"Most animals are lazy. They do not want to work. If they worked harder and had faith in the Free Market, everything would be fine. The Free Market can feed us all, if we believe in it!"

Next day he lays off half his employees.

Rosy the Hog is still President. He got ill when financial depressions hit. Can't walk on his own so a Goat pulls him round in a cart. Tours Capital Farm to see what's what though he's crippled. Food lines everywhere. Unemployed animals wanderin' farm to farm. But the Hog come up with a plan. Changes name of the Farm back. To Capitol Farm. Every Corporation sign is repainted. (This time animals are noticin'.) Rosy pushes spending plans through them Board of Directors. Unemployed animals start workin' fer the Corporation. Buildin' roads, plantin' trees. Lotta money improvin' public parks. Farms start unemployment insurance for animals. Rosy starts a pension so old animals can retire with dignity. Asks for universal care but the Board don't do it. New rules is imposed on banks and companies. Bank can lend five times its reserves. No more than that. Companies gots to keep just one book fer the Corporation and fer investors alike.

Then there's a strike on Dog Farm West. Rosy sends in the Animal Army – to protect them strikers from police! First time in history of the Farm a President protects strikers.

Rich animals call Rosy traitor to his class. Talk about gettin' rid of the Pig. Call reforms "creepin' socialism." In secret Rosy tells 'em to 'cept regulation of business to keep commies and socialists outta power.

But then there's war 'gainst Mr. Wilhelm again. Wilhelm takes Pierre's farm. George asks Capitol Farm fer help again. Wilhelm's Farm is strong but so's Capitol Farm. Now this younger Mr. Wilhelm, he ain't a nice man. Says animals is inferior to human beings. Says Jewish folk ain't no human bein's either but animals, you know, like Mice and Rats. Makes 'em work like animals fer nothin' and skins 'em like animals and uses their skins fer leather. If they can't work, slaughters 'em like animals. But when Wilhelm attacks Farm wagons carryin' supplies to George again, Capitol Farm joins the war again.

Soon as war starts Rosy stops his spendin'. Young animals go into the Army. They gots to. And manufactured goods is now fer the war. Rocky the Greyhound and his friends make money supplyin' the Army – and Mr. George's farm. Took some doin', but them Allies defeat Mr. Wilhelm again. They divide up Wilhelm's farm and occupy it fer years.

Now them what was returnin' from war need education and jobs. Rosy says soldiers won't return to unemployment and poverty quietly. Not after riskin' their lives. Rosy passes laws givin' veterans education and money fer land. Them animals go to town with the money. Biggest boom in the history of Capital Farm. Middle-class animals. 'Course mostly whites get the money. Black animals fight the war but they ain't allowed study or to buy land. Specially blacks in the South. Laws on southern farms is discriminatin' 'gainst blacks. But black animals ain't 'llowed to live 'mong whites in the North, neither. It just ain't a written law.

So havin' won the war and ending the financial crisis, Rosy is really popular. But just as the war's won, he takes sick and dies. Animals cried. Not since Abel was a President so loved. His work lasts a lot of years but Rocky and his friends is gonna destroy it.

Chapter Ten

Generations comes and goes. Cato, Abel, even Rosy done gone. Buried on Mt. Majesty. Capitol Farm's now in a cold war with "Commie Farm." But Commie Farm falls of its own weight, breaks into smaller farms. The cold war winter thaws.

Black animals gain socially. Laws ain't fair but it ain't against the law for blacks to make money. Lot of blacks lives in run-down pens and shacks, and their schools ain't as good as whites'. Capitol Farm is still segregated.

With time animals begin forgettin' President Rosy and the Financial Crisis. A Chihuahua named Prince is elected President. Least that's what Prince says. Some say he steals the election. Anyway, he's President of the Corporation now. His family makes money in oil. Prince's friends want to undo Rosy's reforms. You know, stop spendin' money.

"The Corporation," says Prince in his first speech, "is the problem, not the solution. We need to take the fetters off'n business and allow the free market to work. Animals believe in God. I believe God chose me to be President. We don't need no Corporation interference with anythin'. The Lord will let us know his will."

Prince is close with his Vice President, Wolf named Mack. Mack come in out of the wild. Big Wolf. Also worked in oil. Mack tells the Chihuahua what to say in his speeches.

"The President is elected to lead," he growls, "and no one else can share that power!" Most of us animals is afraid of Mack.

Well, a year after Prince is elected, I mean, a year after he become President, a bomb explodes on Dog Farm North. Kills a hundred animals. Prince blames Mr. Smith, a farmer. Most of us animals is shocked. "Who is Mr. Smith?" we says. "And why does he hate us?"

Hearin' of the attack, Prince and Mack hide out in a cave. Situation stabilized, Prince reads a statement written by Mack:

"This is an attack by human beings upon our animal way of life. The name of our Farm therefore shall no longer be Capitol Farm. It shall once again be called Capital Farm because terrorists are attacking our way of life. Let every sign, government record and history book on the Farm be changed."

"Second, the writ of habeas corpus is suspended. A terrorist is any animal I define as a terrorist. Such is my right as President of the Corporation."

"Third, all scientific research other than weapons research must stop."

"Fourth, since we are now at war, taxes on the wealthy must stop in order to increase freedom."

"Fifth, regulation of businesses will cease, and all unions must disband until further notice, in order to strengthen security. Strong business means a strong Farm."

"Sixth, the Animal Army will attack the Farm of Mr. Smyth, because Mr. Smyth sponsored the terrorists who attacked Dog Farm North."

"Seventh, spending programs sponsored by President Rosy will be terminated. We need God on our side, not the Corporation. The Corporation is the problem."

"Eighth, I ask every animal to spend money during these dark days, even on credit, because if we change our way of life, the terrorists win."

"I ask the Board of Directors to make these points law, and I remind you that any animal who questions what I am asking for is a traitor. May God bless Capital Farm!"

Animals is so shocked by the bomb that they agreed with whatever Prince says. Some begins to say, though, that them terrorists come from the Smith family not from Mr. Smyth's farm. Plus Mr. Smyth got the second largest oil fields in the world. He's rollin' in oil. But Prince and Mack then revealed the real reason for war against Mr. Smyth.

"Smyth mistreats his animals," yaps Prince. "If he mistreats his animals, he will attack us, too – just like the terrorists who killed a hundred of us on Dog Farm North. We must invade Smyth's Farm, or the terrorists will win! You don't want the terrorist to win, do you? If we don't bring the fight to Mr. Smyth the terrorists will bring the fight to us! You don't want them to attack us again, do you? "

When many animals do not believe this reason for invadin' Smyth's Farm, the Chihuahua and the Wolf revealed the real reason behind invadin', once again.

"Smyth has a doomsday device," says Mack in an interview a-foamin' at his mouth. "He will destroy the whole world! If we don't invade Smyth's Farm, he will kill us all!"

This convinces most animals and them Board of Directors that Mr. Smyth is a threat. Nobody noticed the difference between Smith and Smyth. Nobody cared. Preparations is made fer war against Mr. Smyth, though some animals protest. And I was one of 'em.

Now Prince and Mack don't want no draft for the war. 'Course their children ain't in the Army. Rich animals don't fight wars. Army was volunteer. Mostly poor animals what needed a job. Soon the Army is ready. It conquers Mr. Smyth's Farm, Rocky Point, in a week. Mr. Smyth's captured, animals put him on trial and kill him.

But now Smyth's gone, question is, "What do you do with his farm?" His animals spoke diff'rent languages. Got diff'rent religions, too. And they hate each other. So President Prince and Mack come up with a plan. First, they give them oil fields and wells to Rocky's grandson, Ricky. He's a Greyhound too. Second, they gives no-bid contracts fer rebuildin' Rocky Point to Mack's friends 'cause, "That's business," Mack says. Third, any animal what works for Mr. Smyth is executed or eaten. Prince is so happy Capital Farm kills Smyth and takes Rocky Point that he give a speech announcin' "Mission Accomplished!" to the Animal Army. And soldiers cheered, o' course.

Well, the job in Rocky Point ain't over. Local animals hate Capital Farm's soldiers. See 'em as occupiers. Make bombs to kill our soldiers. Mack says our soldiers'll be called liberators, 'fore the invasion. But it ain't that way.

"We need food and water; they give us Bibles," Rocky Point animals says. "Our children need an education. They give us Sunday School! We are not Christians! We are Muslims! Why don't they give us what we need?"

Soon local animals is attackin' Corporation soldiers with land mines. Sometimes killin' other locals over them religious differences, sometimes just competin' fer power. Prince and Mack don't allow funerals fer soldiers dyin' in the war so there ain't no more protests. Deaths of soldiers grows but animals on the Farm doesn't notice. I could see it was civil war on Rocky Point but Mack and Prince say no it ain't.

But facts start comin' in that there ain't no "doomsday device" on Rocky Point.

"Just because it hasn't been found doesn't mean it's not there!" growls Mack at animals askin' about that doomsday thing. "Smyth was going to kill us all!" They never ask him 'bout it again. If they does, Mack could have 'em arrested as terrorists and eaten.

Then it comes out the Army is torturin' prisoners held at Rocky Point. They's held under water 'til they say what we wants 'em to say. Or worse. Public outrage when most animals finds out. Members of them Board of Directors calls fer Prince and Mack to quit but they won't. "Capital Farm does not torture!" Prince says. But the Army keeps doin' it. In the end, Mack blames some privates in the Army fer it, but it was his idea, I think. Them privates is put on trial and goes to jail. Problem seems to go away. Most animals is just tryin' to make a livin'. They doesn't really have time to follow this stuff.

But now them problems Prince's havin' just ain't goin' away. Duck Farm South is at the end of the Ramblin' River. Prince and Mack dam it 'bove Duck Farm. They build the dam but won't pay fer maintenance. Corporation's the problem, as Prince says.

Well, in August a hurricane hit Duck Farm, and the dam burst. Most animals, who's black, is drownded. Entire farm destroyed.

"Act of God," says Mack the Wolf. "That's what it is. I do not think Duck Farm South should be rebuilt."

'Course there's backlash for that. Animals is askin', "What are President Prince and Vice-President Mack doing?"

Year later, second Financial Crisis strikes. Prince and Mack relaxed the regulatin' of banks and done way with reforms started by Rosy. Banks is lendin' one hundred times what they got in reserves. They's allowed to keep four different books, not just one or even two. Company execs makes a thousand times what one animal makes in a year. And most animals is afraid to complain for fear of bein' eaten.

Well, them banks made bad loans so now they can't pay their debts again. No animal can borrow money so businesses is goin' bankrupt, layin' off employees. So now workers can't pay their mortgages so they losin' their farms to foreclosure. So Prince and Mack put Corporation money into the failin' banks. Them banks is supposed to lend money to all us animals but they don't. Well, the Corporation put no conditions on them loans to them banks. Banks use the money to pay their execs a bonus. Average animals can't understand it. But what could they do? The law's the law.

Now 'cause of never-ending war at Rocky Point, suspension of trials and habeas corpuses, destruction of Duck Farm South and the second Financial Crisis, Prince ain't very popular. Some animals says he's worst President in Corporation history. 'Course most animals won't says it fer fear of bein' arrested as terrorists.

Then one mornin', as animals walk to them fields to work, they sees public signs is been changed once again. 'Stead of readin' "Capital Farm," they says "Cannibal Farm" in bright red paint. Just like Mother Nan said.

On Pig Farm South Mack sees them signs and he loses it. Mack attacks one sign with his fangs and pierces his tongue with them splinters. Makes him angrier. Orders police Dogs to arrest suspicious animals on the Farm but neither Mack nor Prince never told us who got arrested or why. Least I never found out.

OTHER FABLES

1. Two Roosters

There was a fight between Tanagran roosters, the kind that fight as hard as men, they say:

The loser hid in a corner of the henhouse, covered with shame and his blood. The winner jumped up to the roof of the henhouse, clapping his wings and crowing loudly.

An eagle snatched him from the roof and carried him off. The loser then approached the hens with no fear, winning the better prize for losing.

So never boast, oh man, when luck lifts you up. Failure may be the cause of your success.

2. The Octopus

There once was an octopus who lived in a coral garden. One day, a ship ran aground on the reef and sank. A golden crown crusted with diamonds, rubies and emeralds sank from the wreck, landing on the ocean floor in the middle of the octopus' garden.

The octopus was quite overjoyed to see the crown and quickly latched onto it with its tentacles, tucking the crown underneath its body. Luckily, no one else had seen the crown fall to the bottom of the sea. The octopus put the crown on its head. It wasn't very comfortable, but the octopus didn't care.

For many days, the octopus sat under its crown, admiring its sparkling gems and golden luster, getting weaker from lack of food. Finally, the octopus was so weak that he became prey to a large moray eel who ate the octopus for lunch and left the octopus' crown where he found it.

3. The Bees

The economy of a local beehive was booming. Spring rains had produced sweet flowers of every fragrance and color for the worker bees to gather nectar to make honey. The nest had seven combs full of golden honey by August. By October, there were ten.

Later, during the winter months when the bees huddled together to keep out the cold and eat stored honey, one worker bee saw how many honey combs there were and asked, "Why can't we have more honey to eat? There's more than enough to go around. It's been a productive year."

"Sshhh!" a chorus of her friends hissed. "We're not allowed to eat any more honey than what the Queen allows."

"What do you want to ask for more honey for, anyway? You want it all for yourself, don't you!?"

"You're going to make trouble for the rest of us workers. Be happy with what She gives you and be quiet for all our sake!"

"I deserve more honey," the worker bee said. "We all do. We gathered nectar all summer. From that nectar we workers made all this honey. I'm going to ask the Queen for more honey!"

She made her way to the court where the Queen was eating, surrounded by her drones. Trembling, the worker approached the throne and bowed low before the Queen. Then she stammered but finally managed to ask the Queen Bee to increase the workers' daily ration of honey, "As there is a surplus, Your Majesty, and we gathered the nectar, to begin with."

The Queen Bee could scarcely believe Her ears! She almost fell off her throne, which was lucky for the drones, who were also eating honey, as She would have squashed one of them. "How dare this nobody, this nothing, ask for more honey! If I don't do something quick, I'll lose everything!" She said to Herself and quickly called for Her royal guards.

"Guards! Guards! Throw her out of My nest!" She thundered, pointing at the unhappy worker, who was shaking even harder with fear.

"On what charge, Your Majesty?"

"Class warfare!" the Queen screamed at the worker bee, who was trying to hide, unsuccessfully, behind her tiny wings. "This will teach the others not to ask for more! I need that honey for Myself and My drones, or to make war... We have banished her! Cast her out!!"

The guards, who did not want their own rations of honey to be cut, were happy to oblige their Queen. They dragged the worker bee out of the court while telling her she was only getting what she deserved for not knowing her place. They dragged her kicking and screaming all the way to the entrance of the beehive, past the other workers who stood by and watched.

The royal guards pushed the worker bee out of the warm hive, out into the cold, gray air. She tried to enter the nest several times, telling the guards she was sorry for what she had done and would never do it again, but the guards would have none of it. They threatened to sting her if she didn't go away.

Finally, when the worker bee saw that her efforts were in vain, she flew off to the eaves of a nearby house where she died of hunger and the cold.

4.   The Fox and the Grapes

On a mountain's side a bunch of grapes hung from a dark-colored vine. Seeing the dark dappled grapes, a clever fox tried to grab the purple fruit with his paws by jumping again and again – because the grapes were really ripe and it was harvest season.

But it was all for nothing because he could not reach the grapes, so he walked off and, disappointed, told himself this lie: "Sour grapes -- not ripe like I thought."

5.   The Horse and the Ass

A man owned a horse which he would lead bare-back while he set his luggage on his old donkey. As the donkey was doing all the work, he approached the horse to speak with him:

"If you would share my burden, I'd be saved. If not, I'm a goner...."

"You keep going!" the other said, and, "Don't annoy me!" he added.

The ass kept working, keeping quiet, but unable to endure his suffering any more, he fell down dead, just as he predicted.

Quickly the master drew the horse up to the dead donkey and, loosing the whole burden, loaded all of the donkey's harness and baggage onto the horse, including the skin of the dead ass, when the master had skinned him.

Said the horse, "My judgment was wrong. I didn't want to share even a little of the burden, and now I'm forced to carry everything."

6. The Man Who had Termites

There once was a man who had a lovely new house made out of wood. He would repair and paint the house whenever it needed work. It was a labor of love for him, so he was especially vexed when termites infested his house and began to destroy it.

Instead of hiring an exterminator, however, the man decided to fight the termites himself. As often as he killed them, more seemed to appear, so he began to look for a source of termites in the area, some kind of nest from which they came.

Across the street from the man's house was an old, worn and dilapidated house where the owners never mowed the lawn and allowed the paint on the house to become cracked. The man decided the termites were coming from the house across the street.

One night, when the people who lived in the old house were away, the man snuck over there and started a fire in the kitchen using gasoline. The fire spread quickly, and soon the entire house was in flames. By the time the fire department arrived, it was too late. By morning, nothing was left of the house but smoldering ash.

Unfortunately, the people who lived in the house across the street had no homeowner's insurance, so they abandoned the house and went to live somewhere else.

The termites did not cease infesting the man's house, however. Try as he might, the man could not get rid of them. And termites were not his only problem. Soon rats infested the ruins of the old house across the street, which was not rebuilt, and then spread to the man's house. So by destroying the house across the street the man not only did not rid himself of the termites but also gave himself rats.

7.   The Hen and the Rooster

There once was a rooster on a prosperous farm. This cock used to bring hens on the farm bits of food so they would mate with him. Sometimes he would nip a tasty bud from a shrub to give to a pretty little hen. The hen would then let him mate with her in return for the food. Everyone was happy with this arrangement, the rooster and all the hens.

Unfortunately, that part of the country experienced a severe drought. As a result, the cock found it increasingly difficult to find food to bring to the hens. There were, however, any number of different rocks and pebbles in and around the farm that looked similar to edible plant buds. The cock presented these to the hens successfully and was able to mate with all of the hens even though he had no buds to give any of them. No one involved would mention that the pebbles were inedible, and things went on quite happily as though there were no drought.

One day, the cock wanted to mate with an older hen who had been around the farm longer than the cock himself had. He presented her with a pebble that did not resemble a bud or leaf even remotely. It was caked with dirt and dust.

"This is too much!" the hen said. "When the pebbles you gave me looked just a little bit like food I was willing to let it go. I know there's a drought, and I don't expect any extra food from you, but if you can't even pretend to bring me a real present, I refuse to mate with you!" So she picked herself up and went home alone.

8.   The Ants and the Termites

There once was a nest of prosperous carpenter ants living in a fallen oak tree. They had evolved so much politically that they did not have a king or queen but held free elections and shared the necessary work among themselves in a genuine meritocracy, giving to each and every ant according to its skill and labor. Some of the ants raised aphids, which they milked for nectar, while others cultivated fungus farms inside the fallen oak tree.

In another fallen oak tree in the same forest, however, was another nest of ants where a Slavemaker Ant ruled. He and his henchmen raided other nests, carrying off the young to make them their slaves. They tortured the ants they oppressed mercilessly, keeping them in a continual state of fear and plundering whatever food they gathered. If the other ants accomplished anything, the Slavemaker took credit for it, although he never did any of the work.

The ants in the second oak tree hated the Slavemaker for oppressing them, but they could never unite against him because they were divided among themselves. If some lone ant resisted the Slavemaker, that ant was tortured to death in the darkest recesses of the fallen oak tree, which the ants called "the dungeons."

In the beginning, the wealthy free nest and the enslaved nest made treaties with each other. In fact, the democratic nest even gave the Slavemaker food and soldiers because he was at war with a common enemy: the termites who allegedly had designs on all the trees of the forest.

Eventually, however, the free nest and the enslaved nest became enemies and went to war with each other. Some said the free ants wanted the fallen oak tree where the Slavemaker ruled for a new colony, but the leaders of the free ants claimed they made war against the Slavemaker in order to free his slaves.

The free ants, being more prosperous and numerous, quickly invaded and subdued the Slavemaker and won the War of the Oak Tree. They put their soldier ants in charge of the Slavemaker's nest and killed only the Slavemaker and his henchmen after putting them on trial. Then they declared the second nest liberated and held free elections.

Unfortunately, once the free ants killed the Slavemaker and his henchmen, no one was left to rule over the newly liberated nest. The formerly enslaved and oppressed ants would not cooperate with each other and began fighting among themselves in civil war according to their ethnicities and religions.

Soon the liberated nest was a writhing mass of ants biting one another. Legs, thoraxes, mandibles – body parts were strewn all through and around the liberated nest. Worse, no one was a clear winner of the civil war, so it just continued.

Caught in the middle of this civil war were the soldier ants from the free nest who attempted to separate the feuding ants by coming between them. The formerly oppressed ants viewed the free ants as enemy occupiers, however, so instead of fighting each other, they attacked the free soldier ants, instead.

At first the leaders of the free ants sent more soldiers to restore order to the liberated nest, but this did not work. The fighting on all sides increased, and the free soldier ants died in great numbers. Eventually, by means of their own elections, the free ants put pressure on their leaders to call all their soldiers back to the free nest in the first oak tree. The soldiers, some of them severely mangled, limped back home to the free nest in a long ant caravan over the sandy floor of the forest.

The termites, now seeing their chance, invaded the liberated nest in great numbers. They killed all the ants there and consumed the second oak tree until it was completely gone.

9.   The Chirping Cricket

One sultry summer night, a beautiful songbird asked the single cricket in her tree, "Why do you make such a chirping racket all night long? By summer's end, cricket, you will be dead, while we songbirds go on living for many, many years with our mates. What have you got to be happy about? How can you sing?"

"It's true," the cricket said, "by summer's end, my friends and I will be no more. But I'm going to keep making music -- as long as I'm alive -- and next summer, when my voice is gone, they'll be new crickets chirping in my place in this very tree because I'm singing here now."

10. The Lion and the Owl

After many years of ruling and reigning, a lion visited the wise owl who lived in the forest and had a particular reputation for wisdom among the animals.

"Oh, wise owl," the lion said, "what is the meaning of life?"

The owl said nothing, however, but just sat on a branch in its tree, sleeping.

The lion, assuming the owl must be gathering its thoughts together on such a subject, waited patiently for the owl to speak. After ten minutes of awkward silence, the lion spoke again.

"I have traveled quite far. I left my family and my home. My strength is not what it used to be, and I know my life will be over soon. Will you not tell me the meaning of life?"

Again, the owl said nothing. But the lion was patient. He did not lose his temper. He waited all night and all day for the owl to speak. He did not leave the spot where was sitting, not even to get a drink though he was thirsty. Finally, at sunset the following day, the lion spoke again.

"This is the third and final time I will speak," the lion said. "If you say nothing I will simply leave. Please, wise owl, tell me: What is the meaning of life?"

"Who?" said the owl. "Who?"

"Yes!" the lion exclaimed. "That's it! I have been asking the wrong question all these years! Thank you, wise owl! Thank you so much!"

The lion went home to his pride, and when a younger male lion eventually pushed him out of the pride, he walked off alone to die in the wilderness with peace of mind.

11. The Chameleon's Complaint

A chameleon was resting on a tree branch one day when a snake came sliding by. Quickly the chameleon changed brown to escape detection. The snake passed by, and the chameleon exclaimed, "Being brown is the worst thing that could have ever happened to me! My life is ruined!"

Later that day, the chameleon was resting on a tropical leaf when another snake came sliding by. The chameleon turned as green as the leaf, and the snake, slithering on, was never the wiser. "Awful!" the chameleon wept. "I'm the unluckiest person in the whole world! I hate green!"

Finally, that same day, the chameleon was crawling across some yellow sand. "I refuse to turn the color of dirt!" the chameleon said to himself. He crawled over the yellow sand as fast as he could but was visible because he was still green. A bird, however, saw him and swallowed him whole.

What color is the chameleon now?

12. The Oak and the Reeds

Wind, taking an oak tree from a mountain, deposited it in a river. Rapids carried it downstream, a gigantic organism from the past. Many calamus reeds stood on either side of the river, drinking water from the river at their leisure.

The oak was in shock: How could such a frail, powerless plant survive the storm while she, such a great oak, was torn out by the roots?

The calamus wisely said, "Don't be shocked: You lost battling the winds, but we are bent by benign reason, and, if at all, the breeze only sways our heads." Thus the calamus. This story shows that it is not necessary to battle the powerful, but to yield.

13. A Dog Carrying Meat Across the River

A dog stole a piece of meat from a chef and then crossed a stream. Having seen the meat's shadow in the stream, he dropped the flesh and charged its shadow because it was bigger than the meat.

However, he got neither that "meat" nor the meat which he discarded, and he forded the stream back to the chef's kitchen, still hungry.

An uncertain life to every avaricious man, wasted in empty hope of gain.

14. The Fir Tree and the Thorn Bush

A silver pine tree and a bramble bush debated each other. The silver pine praised herself in manifold ways: "I am beautiful and my measurements are well-proportioned. I reach up so high that I make my home among the clouds. I am a pillar holding up the roof and the keel of a ship. How could you, a thistle, argue with such a tree?"

The thorn bush said to her, "If you were to remember the axes that continually cut you down, even you would prefer to be a bramble bush."

Every successful person not only has greater glory than lesser people but also suffers more trials.

15. The Boy and the Whale

A boy who loved animals and wanted to become a veterinarian went on a whale-watching expedition. The people on the day-trip saw many wonderful sea creatures, including a large blue whale who dove and breached to the crowd's delight.

Yet the whale was old, and shortly after the whale-watching expedition was over, the old whale died, and his body sank to the bottom of the ocean. Some cuttlefish, bacteria and bottom-feeders began to eat the corpse, until no flesh was left on his giant whale bones.

The boy went home after the whale-watching expedition, and that night, as he fell asleep, he remembered the great flukes and the spouts of water in the air.

Once asleep, the boy dreamt of the whale swimming, but he never dreamt of the old whale's body lying on the sandy bed of the ocean or of the silent scavengers feasting on the old whale's flesh.

16. The Orchid and the Wasps

There once was a Tongue Orchid who smelled , of course, just like a female wasp, and whose flower looked like the comely body of a female wasp. A male wasp, flying by and smelling the aphrodisiacal scent, landed on the Tongue Orchid and, thinking the flower was a female wasp, proceeded to mate with the Tongue Orchid.

Finally, after working up his passion, the male wasp climaxed, ejaculating his sperm into the flower, pollinating the Orchid without knowing it.

Flying up from the flower, the male wasp met an actual female wasp who was looking for a mate herself.

"You're too late," said the male as she smiled at him, "for I just mated with this sexy female and am all spent!" And he flew off dizzily to find some sleep.

The female wasp, landing on the Tongue Orchid, didn't see a rival female wasp anywhere.

"What is wrong with males these days?" she said. "I'm a perfectly good female, and they're not at all interested! Why wouldn't he mate with me?"

The Tongue Orchid said nothing.

17. The Hen in the Pen

A chicken once lived in a cage not much bigger than herself. She was not allowed to stretch her legs or walk around the yard. A poultry company bred her for the slaughter, so she was forced to lie in her own excrement, because it saved the company money.

One day, another hen, a relative from the country, came to visit the hen in her pen. Of course it was a very dangerous journey to make, for if the poultry company found the unauthorized visitor, it would put her in a cage, too, and her fate would be no better than her cousin's. She had heard of her cousin's plight, so she decided to visit her and to see the situation for herself.

"My cousin," she whispered through the bars of the cage, "you must escape from here!"

"And where shall I go?" said the hen in her pen. "The humans are everywhere. Whether I go or stay , my fate will be the same."

"The farm where I live is not like this," the visitor urged. "I walk around all day and get to lay eggs. Yes, I will probably be eaten by some humans, eventually, but now I have my dignity. My cousin, you must come with me!"

And so the cousin from the country picked the lock on the hen's cage, but it still did not make any difference. The hen's leg muscles had so atrophied from staying in her cage all the time that she was completely unable to walk. Her cousin therefore left her in the cage and went back to the country, weeping, rather than being caught, too.

18. Cuttlefish in Love

A large male cuttlefish guarded his female jealously on the bottom of the ocean. He stared down two rivals, flashing them a warning, changing his color to threatening colors like bright yellow, orange and red.

While he was distracted, a smaller male cuttlefish floated by him unnoticed and, changing his color to match that of the female, joined with the female and began to mate with her.

After scaring off his two rivals, the large male noticed a change in his female. She was larger than he remembered her, and her shape was unusual. Moving closer, he saw the small male, at which point the small male darted away.

Quickly the large male seized a crab traveling across the ocean bottom and presented it to his mate. She ate it gladly, and the large male cuttlefish was happy that his dominance over her had been acknowledged and restored.

19. Farmer and Cranes

Cranes were eating up the land of a farmer in which he had sown grains of wheat. For a long time he drove them off by swinging an empty sling to frighten them away.

When they suffered nothing from his slinging of the air, they spurned him and stopped flying away.

Finally he stopped what he was doing, and slinging stones now, he hit most of the cranes with rocks.

As they were leaving the field, they shrieked to each other, "Let's escape to the land of pygmies. This man isn't pretending to frighten us anymore; he's actually doing something!"

20. Wolf and Crane

Whoever decides to serve a bad person for wages makes two mistakes: First, because he aids the unworthy, and second, since he cannot safely withdraw.

A bone swallowed by a wolf lodged in his throat. The pain too great, he offered a reward to anybody to extract the damn thing.

Finally, a female crane, persuaded by promises, performed a dangerous operation by sticking her neck as far as she could down into the wolf's gullet.

When she demanded remuneration according to the agreement, he replied, "Ingrate! You took your head safely out of my mouth and you expect an *extra* reward!"

21. Rabbits and Frogs

The rabbits did not want to live any more. They unanimously decided to throw themselves into the black water of the lake because they were the weakest of all living things, cowards at heart and knowing how to do nothing except running away.

When they came up to the wide water's edge they beheld a group of frogs there who immediately crouched down and sprang off into the deep mud to get away.

They stood there, watching, and one, finding his will to live, said, "Let's go now. There's no use dying – I see others weaker than us."

22. Wolf and Sheep

To the selfsame river the wolf and a sheep came to drink. The wolf stood upstream, and the sheep farther off downstream.

Then, with his evil maw, the quick robber tried to pick a fight. "Why," he says, "have you sullied my drinking water?"

"How could I do that, wolf? Down from you to me the water flows."

Put off by the power of honesty, he said, "Six months ago, you cursed at me!"

"I wasn't even born yet."

"Then by the god of strength, your father cursed at me!" he said, and he snatched up the sheep in his mouth, tore him and killed him for no good reason.

This fable is for those who abuse the innocent on manufactured grounds.

23. Stag at the Fountain

What is despised is often more useful than what is praised, I have found. This narrative is witness.

When he had drunk, a stag stood by the fountain and watched his reflection in the water. Seeing his branching horns there, he praised them and criticized his excessively slender legs, but then he was scared out of his wits by the yell of hunters, so he fled across an open field and quickly eluded the dogs.

Then he reached a tangled wood, in which his horns caught in the branches, so the dogs started to tear into him with their cruel teeth.

As he died, he said, "O unhappy me! Who never found out how needful were my limbs which I hated – and what grief those that I praised held.

24. Bird and Cat

Once upon a time, a bird became ill. Bending over her, a cat said, "How are you? Do you need anything? I'll take of everything. You just let me save you."

"Just leave me alone," she said, "and I will survive."

25. Fox and Crow

A carrion-crow who had taken cheese in his mouth was standing in a tree. A wily fox, wanting the cheese, tricked the bird using this fiction: "Your wings are lovely, Crow, your eyesight sharp and your plumage spectacular! You vaunt an eagle's chest, with your claws you dominate the beasts! Mute, you do not caw – and what a bird you are!"

The crow at heart was puffed up by this praise. Spitting the cheese out of his mouth, he cawed and cawed and cawed.

The clever fox seized the cheese and gave the crow a tongue-lashing, "You aren't dumb – you really can speak, Crow! You really do have every positive trait that a bird can have – except, of course, good sense!'

26. Cow and She-Goat, Sheep and Lion

Partnering up with the powerful is never safe. This fable confirms my opinion.

Cow, she-goat and sheep (always tolerant though wronged) became partners with a lion in a leafy ravine. When they caught a giant stag, lion divided the take: "I get the first share because I am called a king by name. You will confer the second share on me because I am your partner. Then the third goes to me because I am stronger and something bad will happen to whoever mentions the fourth share…"

Thus evil took the whole prize for itself.

27. The Peacock Sings

In order to strengthen their community, the animals of the forest began giving performances in the cool of the evening.

Several birds sang at concerts, so it occurred to the turtledove to ask the peacock to sing as well. "The peacock should have the most beautiful of voices," she said, "since the peacock is the most beautiful bird!"

Finally, the evening arrived for the concert. Even the fox showed up, sitting in the back of the audience of animals, while birds sat in the branches of the trees.

The peacock soon came on stage, beautiful to behold in its glory, and the animals cheered, expecting the best show ever.

Then the peacock began to sing a song and its voice was a terrible shrieking, painful to listen to. All the animals ran or flew away as fast as they could.

Except for the fox. He still sat at the back of the clearing.

"Aren't you frightened by my singing," said the peacock.

"No," he said. "I'm not."

"Why not?" said the peacock.

"Because I know," the fox said, "that looks aren't everything but they do mean something."

28.   Wolf and Fox Judged by the Monkey

Whoever is known for a single fraud, even though he also tells the truth, is never believed after. This short story by Aesop shows that.

Wolf accused fox of the crime of thievery. She denied the accusation, and a chimpanzee sat as judge between them.

When each had made his or her case, the chimp read his verdict: "You didn't suffer loss of anything to sue for, Wolf; and Fox, you, I know, stole whatever property may be in your possession."

29.   The Old Bull and the Young Steer

A young steer grazing free in the fields, who never wore a yoke, yelled at a nearby bull struggling in front of his plough, "Pitiful! You have such an awful life!"

The bull said nothing, however, and ploughed on.

But when the locals decided to make sacrifice to the gods they unyoked the old bull and put him out to pasture. But they roped the wild young bull by the horns and dragged him to the altar to spill his blood. And the old bull said to the other, "For this you were kept in reserve from working. The young one races past his elder. First prize: To die as a sacrifice! Your youth will not be worn down gradually under a yoke, but momentarily under an axe!"

30. Fox Trapped Under a Tree

An old oak had a hole in its root system. There sat a goatherd's old beat-up leather bag filled with stale bread and spoiled meat. Scampering down into the hole, a fox ate up all the contents of the bag. As was only right, her belly ballooned up with food, but the hole was so narrow she could not squeeze back out.

Another fox, happening upon her and seeing how she cried, said, "Stay put until you're starving. You won't come out of there until you have the very same girth you went in with."

31. Nature's Boy

A man in financial difficulties walked along the agitated ocean shore while the wind blew waves white in autumn gusts of thirty to forty miles per hour. The sky immediately overhead was overcast with cloud, but in the distance he saw patches of bright October blue between cumulous clouds puffing bright white.

He saw autumn leaving, red, yellow and brown, on trees losing their green summer glory, and felt cool oxygen fill his stale lungs.

"I am in pain," he said aloud to the clouds gliding serenely in the sky. "Everything brings me pain, and it does not seem fair."

He stood on the sand and gazed in the distance. The sun shone beautiful on far-away hills, undulating rills of water swept white by wind mirroring the expanse of firmament spreading in all directions overhead.

And seeing these things he realized he didn't know everything there was to know, didn't feel everything there was to feel, and the pain just went away.

32.   The Jackass and the Old Shepherd

For the poor nothing changes but the names of politicians when the administration changes. This little fable indicates that.

An aged coward pastured his donkey in his meadow. Terrified at the sudden shout of an enemy, he told his jackass to run away so as not to be captured. That tough animal told him, "I ask you – do you really suppose the winner of this fight will load two packs on my back?"

"No," said the old man.

"So what does it matter to me whom I work for if I carry only one pack at a time?"

33.   The Bitch in Labor

The compliments spoken by an evil man spring a trap which this verse counsels us how to avoid.

A pregnant bitch asked another bitch if she could birth her brood in the other's hole, and she readily agreed. Then when she asked for her place back, the mother requested a brief extension, until her puppies were strong enough to conduct away. When said time elapsed, she began to demand her bed more vehemently.

"If you are as strong as my gang and me," the bitch said, "I'll give you the place."

34. The Lion in Love

A lion asked to marry a man's young daughter, and the old man, showing no bad feeling or secret hatred, said, "I'll gladly give you a wedding: Who wouldn't want to marry into the lion's family? But, you know, the minds of virgins and children are weak. How long your claws are, how big your fangs are to us! What bride would fold you in her arms unafraid? What person seeing you would not scream? Watch out, if you want to marry! Don't be a wild beast. Be a bridegroom."

Beside himself with happiness and believing the man's words, the lion pulled his teeth and trimmed his claws with a knife. Then he showed himself to his father-in-law and begged the daughter. Then each attacked the lion, one with a club, another throwing a rock, and he lay prone, dying like a pig, taught by a tricky old-timer a lesson in wisdom: People and lions don't mix.

A man unknowingly hurts himself when he tries to share in those things which are not natural.

35. Crabby Example

"Do not walk sideways," mother crab said to her son. "Do not pull your legs slantways over this wet rock!"

He said, "You are my teacher, Mother: You walk in a straight line first, and, seeing you, I'll do the same."

36. The Lion and the Mouse

The lion caught a mouse meaning to eat it.

The domestic thief, nearing his doom, squeaked out wretchedly for his life: "Better for you to fatten your belly hunting the meat of stags and bulls with great big horns! A mouse isn't enough to smack your lips over! I beg you to spare me! Perhaps I will return the favor, though I am tiny!"

The great beast laughed aloud and let the beggar live, but later, attacking some avid hunters, he was captured in a net and tied.

Then the mouse slipped secretly from his hole and, with his tiniest of teeth, he chewed through the massive rope. He freed the lion, paying him back for saving his life.

The moral of the story is clear to those who think: Save the poor and don't give up on them, since even a mouse freed a captured lion.

37. The Bull and the Lion

Once upon a time, a lion invited a wild ox to dinner, pretending to make sacrifice to the mother of the gods, but in reality plotting against the bull's life. Not suspecting anything, the ox gave his word to attend.

When he reached the lion's house, the ox stood outside the lion's doors, eyeing the many pots brim-full of boiling water together with the polished knives and the cleavers used to skin cattle – all in the front courtyard. Outside by the gate there was no animal except a small chicken tethered to a post, so the ox rushed off, fleeing to a nearby mountain.

Later, the lion blamed the ox when he met him.

"I really did show up," the bull answered, "and here's what I saw: You're sacrifice was much too puny for your kitchen!"

38. The Seagull

A white seagull dying of hunger flew to the north shore of Long Island looking for food. He seized a mollusk in his bill at low tide and flew over the beach parking lot to drop the prize onto the pavement below, cracking it open, but he never got the chance to eat anything. Two other seagulls, one white, one brown, flew after him, trying to take away his food.

Try as he might, the hungry gull could not shake the other two. When he rose, they rose. When he dove, they followed.

Finally the hungry gull flew back to the water in frustration and seized three mollusks this time in his large bill. Once over the pavement again, he let all three mollusks fall to the ground, breaking the shells on the blacktop. Each of the three gulls then seized his prize and ate his dinner.

Flying away full, the once-hungry gull said to himself, "I had to finally get something in my stomach, so it was worth feeding those two. But now that I'm satisfied, I won't be spending the rest of my day feeding those lazy bastards! Let them get their own food -- I'm leaving!"

www.ingramcontent.com/pod-product-compliance
Lightning Source LLC
Chambersburg PA
CBHW071413170626
46811CB00003B/1390

* 9 780615 627939 *